# Nurses to Brides

*The Peniglatt sisters find their*
*happily-ever-afters when wedding bells ring!*

The Peniglatt sisters
couldn't be more different—
Kira is Miss Responsible, whilst Krissy is
the family wild child! Their only similarity is
their total dedication to caring for others.

These hard-working nurses
don't have much time for love. Until
two very special men walk into their lives,
determined to sweep them off their feet!

*The Doctor She Always Dreamed Of*

Can Derrick tempt Kira to believe in for ever?

and

*The Nurse's Newborn Gift*

Will single mum Krissy let Spencer
into her life…and her heart?

You won't want to miss this
sexy and emotional duet
from the fabulous Wendy S. Marcus!

Dear Reader,

I'm thrilled to be back with two brand-new Medical Romances about Kira and Krissy Peniglatt—two very special sisters who work hard to care for and give to others without expecting anything in return.

In *The Doctor She Always Dreamed Of* Kira is a no-nonsense professional, working on the business side of nursing. Rather than enjoying the glitz and glamour of New York City, she divides her time between her job as Director of Case Management at a large insurance carrier and caring for her severely brain-injured mother. With no time to spare, she gave up on finding love a long time ago. But she's never met a man like Dr Derrick Limone—a man willing to do anything to spend time with her.

In *The Nurse's Newborn Gift* Krissy is a laid-back travelling nurse who's in the process of changing her carefree life to keep a promise to her dead best friend—a soldier killed in the war. Having his baby, giving his parents the gift of a grandchild they can dote on and love in his absence, may seem extreme to some—but not to Krissy. She's waited five years, and she's ready to do it all on her own. But Spencer Penn, the baby's godfather, has other ideas.

I hope you enjoy reading Kira's and Krissy's stories as much as I enjoyed writing them! To find out about my other books visit WendySMarcus.com.

Wishing you all good things,

*Wendy S. Marcus*

# THE DOCTOR
# SHE ALWAYS
# DREAMED OF

BY
WENDY S. MARCUS

First published in Great Britain 2016
By Mills & Boon, an imprint of HarperCollins*Publishers*
1 London Bridge Street, London, SE1 9GF

Large Print edition 2017

© 2016 Wendy S. Marcus

ISBN: 978-0-263-06679-1

Our policy is to use papers that are natural, renewable and recyclable products and made from wood grown in sustainable forests. The logging and manufacturing processes conform to the legal environmental regulations of the country of origin.

Printed and bound in Great Britain
by CPI Antony Rowe, Chippenham, Wiltshire

3390121x

**Wendy S. Marcus** is an award-winning author of contemporary romance who lives in the beautiful Hudson Valley region of New York, where she spends way too much time indoors on her computer. Writing. Really! Okay…more like where she spends way too much time on Twitter and Facebook! To learn more about Wendy, and the books she's managed to write in spite of her social media addiction, visit WendySMarcus.com.

Visit the Author Profile page at millsandboon.co.uk for more titles.

This book is dedicated to my cousin,
Justine De Leon, in honour of her
becoming a US citizen. We love you
and we're so happy you're here!

With special thanks to Barbara Kram for
helping me run through some HMO insurance
fraud scenarios. Any errors are my own.

Thank you to my wonderful editor, Flo Nicoll,
for always pushing me to do my best.

And thank you to my family,
for supporting me in all that I do.

### Praise for
### Wendy S. Marcus

'Wendy S. Marcus is a special author for
me… Read this and you'll get an enthralling
contemporary love story.'

—*Goodreads* on
*Craving Her Soldier's Touch*

'If you are looking for a read that will have
you laughing, crying and sighing, while being
swept up in sweet yet hot romance, I highly
recommend *Craving Her Soldier's Touch*.'

—*Goodreads*

'If you are looking for a smart, sexy,
heart-warming contemporary medical romance
that is hard to put down, I highly recommend
you try *Tempting Nurse Scarlet*!'

—*Goodreads* on
*NYC Angels: Tempting Nurse Scarlet*

# CHAPTER ONE

"I WANT TO speak to the man in charge."

Kira Peniglatt closed her eyes and pinched the bridge of her nose. "You've reached the *woman* in charge," she told the angry older gentleman on the telephone who'd been yelling at her and making unreasonable demands for the past ten minutes. "I'm the Director of Case Management here at We Care Health Care."

No sooner were the words out of her mouth than she regretted them. *When talking with disgruntled customers, must remember to use WCHC instead.*

"We Care Health Care," he mimicked. "What a crock!"

If she had a dollar for every time she'd heard that or something similar over the past five years, she'd be a wealthy woman, retired at the age of thirty, living by a lake or a beach, somewhere far away from the crowds and smells of New York City. This job she now hated, her tightwad boss, and harassing phone calls from angry people would be nothing more than a distant, unpleasant memory.

"You don't care about me," the husband of client Daisy Limone went on. "And you sure as hell don't care about my wife or you'd be sending someone to help me take care of her. I can't do it all by myself. Three days in and my back is aching from all the lifting, my knees are swelled up from all the bending, and my hips are on fire from running up and down the stairs all day."

Kira wanted to scream, "You brought this on yourself you ornery old man, now deal with it!" But she'd always prided herself on her professionalism, regardless of the challenging circumstances. Lately circumstances had become quite challenging.

By pulling his wife—she glanced at her computer screen: Primary diagnosis: cerebrovascular accident with residual right-sided hemiparesis and expressive aphasia. Secondary diagnoses: hypertension, osteoporosis, and hypothyroidism—out of an inpatient rehabilitation facility, against medical advice, nine days into an authorized twenty-eight-day stay, he'd assumed full responsibility for her care. Before the patient's stroke she'd filled out a Health Care Proxy designating her husband as her health care agent, giving him complete control over decision-making should her doctor determine she was unable to act on her own behalf—which she wasn't. As a result, there'd been nothing the hospital staff could do.

"Mr. Limone, your wife wasn't ready to come home." He'd underestimated the amount of care she would require, despite being warned—according to hospital documentation—by the case manager, the social worker, a head nurse, and the patient's physical and occupational therapists. "Research shows, after a stroke, patients who attend independent rehabilitation facilities for intensive rehabilitation, before returning home, show much more improvement than those who don't."

"She wasn't happy there, Miss Peniglatt. She put up a fuss every time they tried to take her to therapy. She wouldn't eat or drink." Now, rather than an ornery old man, he sounded like a concerned old man in love with his wife, desperate to help her. "They were threatening to put a tube in her stomach. Neither of us wanted that. She kept saying, 'home'. She'd squeeze my hand and look into my eyes and say, 'home.' Over and over. So I took her home."

Kira's heart went out to him, really, it did. But there was nothing more she could do. "Your insurance plan won't pay for round the clock care in the home setting."

"Who's asking for round the clock? Millie James up the street, her mama's got an aide six hours a day, seven days a week, and she don't need nowhere near as much help as my Daisy."

"Do you have any family—"

"My boys don't live around here. And they're busy. They got their own lives."

*Family takes care of family.* Kira's mother had been telling her that, and Kira had been doing it, for as long as she could remember.

"Is there any other insurance coverage we could help you explore?" she asked.

"We don't have no other insurance. All we have is We Care Health Care. And we need for you to do what your ad says and be there for us when we need you. We need you!"

When marketing had proposed a change to We Care Health Care, We'll Be There When You Need Us, Kira had voiced her concern that the slogan might feed into unrealistic patient expectations. Case in point. "Then can you afford to pay privately for a personal care aide? I could—"

"Why should I have to pay for an aide when I've been paying you every month for years?"

He made it sound like he paid her directly. "Mr. Limone, you pay for medical insurance coverage that does not include custodial care such as bathing and dressing provided by personal care aides," Kira said, trying to keep calm. "What about a friend or a neighbor? Have you asked around? Maybe—"

"You sit there in your fancy office," he snapped, "trying to think up ways to get out of paying for the stuff you should be paying for. Then you count up the huge profits you make by withholding care from people who need it and divide the money up into big end-of-year bonus checks. You're a thief! How the hell do you sleep at night?"

Kira inhaled then exhaled. *Don't let him get to you. You do your best. You sleep fine at night.* No she didn't.

"Mr. Limone, as I explained earlier, your insurance coverage is Medicare HMO. Medicare pays for short term, intermittent, skilled care. It does not pay for personal care for bathing and dressing. We contracted with a Medicare Certified Home Health Care Agency in your area."

With a few clicks of her mouse she brought up Mrs. Limone's plan of care. "A nurse came to your home to evaluate your wife. She developed a plan of care that included physical, occupational and speech therapy visits. This plan of care was approved by your wife's physician."

Odd that no home health aide hours were recommended considering the amount of skilled services required, Kira jotted herself a note to call the agency to follow up on that.

"Well it sure as hell wasn't approved by me!" Mr. Limone yelled. "That nurse was in and out of here in under fifteen minutes. Said Daisy wasn't eligible for an aide. How could she not be eligible? She can't get out of bed by herself or eat by herself or dress herself. And since that nurse left, no one's been here. Now she don't return my calls. You need to come up here yourself to see what I'm dealing with. I can send someone to getcha."

"Just because I haven't come to visit your home to see your wife for myself, does not mean I don't care. And it doesn't mean I don't know what is going on up there, either. My office is located a good four hours from you. I am responsible for the case management of, as of this morning, four hundred and thirty-seven patients." The highest her census had ever been.

"That's why we work with your wife's physician and contract with medical providers in your local area for home care evaluations to determine patient care requirements. If you feel there's been an acute change in your wife's health status since the nurse visited three days ago or if you are no longer willing or able to safely care for her at home, you need to dial 911 immediately and have her taken to—"

"Then your boss," he interrupted. "Put me through to your boss."

It was all Kira could do to keep from laughing. Her new, focused-on-the-bottom-line boss—the main reason she now hated her job—could care less about patient care and customer satisfaction, which put him and Kira in close to constant conflict, day in and day out, for months. It was exhausting.

Despite all of the letters that came after her name, MSN—Master's of Science in Nursing, MBA—Master's in Business Administration, and

CCM—Certified Case Manager, the letters RN, for Registered Nurse, were the most important to Kira. They were the reason she always put patients first, the reason she sometimes had to get creative to maintain her patients safely in their homes. She could almost hear the CEO's booming voice when he'd found out she'd agreed to reimburse a home health aide for mileage to get her to travel to a difficult to serve area. *Guidelines for a reason. Cost containment...cut spending... budget...bottom line...blah, blah, blah...*

Case managers straddled the line that separated compassionate patient advocacy and fiscal accountability to their employer. A job made increasingly more difficult with the stringent utilization review and cost constraints of managed care.

"I report to the CEO. He doesn't accept calls from customers. However, we do have an appeals process I'd be happy to have my assistant initiate for you. Or, if you feel my staff or I have in any way treated you unprofessionally, we have a complaint process, which my assistant will also be happy to initiate for you. Let me transfer you now."

Without giving him a chance to argue, she transferred the call. Then she leaned back, let out a breath, and counted to ten.

She'd made it to seven when her office door opened to reveal her assistant, Connie. Her short black hair gelled into random spikes, a tight red blouse and black skirt clinging to her ample curves, and sexy black ankle boots—with silver chains. And a frown on her pretty, round face. "That was mean." She crossed her arms under her well-endowed breasts.

"You could not possibly have filled out the questionnaire for Mr. Limone's complaint and/ or appeal in that short a time," Kira pointed out.

"I put him on hold so I could come in and yell at you."

A pint-sized dynamo, as entertaining as she was efficient, Kira loved her assistant and didn't know what she'd do without her. "I'll make it up to you tonight. Drinks are on me."

That brought a smile to Connie's face. "Good,

because after the week you've had, I plan on us doing a lot of drinking."

Typically, during the few times they'd managed to go out for drinks over the past three years, Connie got drunk and Kira—ever responsible Kira—made sure she got home safely. "Your roommate's okay with me crashing on your couch tonight?" Her sister Krissy home for a rare visit, Kira would be giving up Mom duty for one whole night. Her insides tingled with glee. One night to do anything she wanted. One night to sleep without Mom waking her up, without jumping up at the slightest sound, worried Mom might try to get out of bed by herself and fall.

"She is," Connie said. "But, honey, if I have my way, you won't need to be sleeping on my couch." She winked.

"Yeah, yeah," Kira said. "Because I'm so the type to have an illicit one-night stand with a stranger." Regardless of how much she may want to, that's how women wound up dead.

Connie's phone rang out at her desk. "Shoot." She snapped her fingers. "I came in here to tell you Mr. Limone's son is on the phone. I hope you appreciate the fact that I came in here, in person, to warn you rather than just sending the call in here."

Like Kira had done to her. "You're the best assistant ever." Kira smiled. Then she glanced at the clock. "It's not even noon. Will this day ever end?"

"Do you want me to tell him you're busy?"

Kira shook her head. He'd only call back...even angrier for being put off. She'd learned that earlier this morning. Connie turned to leave.

"Do me a favor?" Kira asked.

"Anything for you." Connie turned back around with a smile. "Legal or illegal, I'm your girl."

Kira smiled back, no doubt in her mind Connie meant it. "A cup of decaf, please."

"With a shot of Baileys?" Connie asked, hopefully. "I might have some random single serving bottles in my desk drawer," she looked up toward the ceiling innocently, "that I received for Christmas and may have forgotten to bring home."

Coffee and Baileys, Kira's favorite. "Get out."

She pointed to the door. "Stop putting unprofessional thoughts in my head and send me my call."

Connie shook her head and let out a disappointed sigh.

"Oh," Kira said. "And when you're done with Mr. Limone senior, would you call Myra Douglas from In Your Home Health Care Services?" Their preferred Certified Home Health Care Agency for the West Guilderford area in upstate New York, where Daisy Limone lived. "Ask her why there are no home health aide services on Daisy Limone's plan of care." Even a few hours a few times a week was better than nothing.

"Sure thing, boss," Connie said. Then with a salute she turned and left, closing the door behind her.

A few seconds later, Kira's phone rang. With a deep fortifying breath—because Mr. Limone junior was even more obnoxious than Mr. Limone senior—she answered it. "Hello, Mr. Limone. I just got off the phone with your father. Before you say one word, let me remind you of our last conversation. The first time you threaten to sue me or curse at me or call me unflattering names I am hanging up this phone. Now what can I do for you?"

"Doctor," he said.

"Excuse me?"

"*Dr.* Limone. I'm a different son."

*God help me, there are two of them.*

"Three actually," he said, his voice deep and tinged with a bit of humor.

Oops. She must have said that out loud.

Thank goodness Connie chose that moment to return with the coffee.

"What can I do for you, *Dr.* Limone?" She took a sip, smiled at her wonderful assistant and mouthed, "Thank you." Although the coffee wasn't near as satisfying without the Baileys.

"I'm calling to apologize, on behalf of my family. Our father can be…difficult."

So could his brother.

"But he's our father," *Dr.* Limone said. "He worked three jobs to keep a roof over our heads and see that all three of us went to college. While he worked, Mom managed the house, the finances and us boys. They got into a routine that's worked for them for fifty-four years. Since Mom's stroke, Dad's struggling to adjust. He doesn't do change very well."

Not many people did. Kira understood that. But, "You know HIPPA regulations don't allow me to discuss Mrs. Limone's care without a signed authorization."

"Please," he said. "As a professional courtesy."

In the past, on a rare occasion, Kira might have given in to a request for a professional courtesy— the unwritten understanding between doctors, nurses and the like to relax the rules of confidentiality a little bit for other health care professionals. But with all the problems she'd been having with her new boss, and with the Limones having an attorney in the family, Kira would be following company procedure to the letter. "I'm sorry, Mr. Limone. Not even as a professional courtesy. Get me a HIPPA release, signed by your father, as your mother's health care agent, specifically giving me authorization to discuss her medical status and treatment with you, by name, and then I'll be happy to speak with you."

"You're just putting me off."

"What I'm doing is following procedure which requires a signed HIPPA release, on file, designating who my staff and I may talk to regarding any specific patient, other than the patient and/ or his or her physician." And just because she was in a bad mood she added, "As a physician you should be familiar with HIPPA regulations, *Dr.* Limone."

"The plan of care is inadequate," he yelled.

If the patient was still in the rehabilitation hospital, she'd be getting the round the clock care and supervision she required. "I can't discuss this with you."

"All I want is for you to explain why no home health aide services were authorized. And why hasn't therapy started yet?"

Kira would be looking into both as soon as she could get off the phone. "I can't discuss this with you."

"Damn it!"

"Get me a signed HIPPA release," Kira said.

"How the hell do you suggest I do that? My practice has exploded. Even working eighty hour weeks I can't get everything done that I need to get done. I live three hours from my parents' house. They don't have a fax machine or a scanner or even e-mail."

"You graduated from medical school," Kira said. "Which means you must be a pretty smart guy. I'm sure you'll figure something out."

Dr. Limone slammed something close to his phone, the sound loud in Kira's ear. "You have no idea how frustratingly difficult this is," he yelled again.

"Yes," Kira said. "I do." From a professional standpoint and from personal experience.

He let out a weary breath. "I'm worried about my dad," he said, sounding exhausted. "He's not in good health. I'm worried about him or my mother falling and getting hurt because they don't have the help they need in the home."

"I understand your concern," Kira said. "From

everything I've heard and read, I think you have every reason to be concerned."

"Yet you're doing nothing to ensure my mother's safety," Dr. Limone yelled.

"This case was just brought to my attention yesterday afternoon."

"My mother is not a *case*, Miss Peniglatt. She's a sweet, kind, loving woman lying helpless in her bed with no one but my elderly father to take care of her because *you* won't authorize an aide."

Kira came dangerously close to losing it. "It is not the responsibility of Medicare or WCHC, as your mother's Medicare HMO, to provide round the clock, in home care. Family takes care of family, Dr. Limone." It's why Kira needed the large salary this job paid her and why she rarely had a free moment to herself. *Family takes care of family.* Kira had grown up watching her mother live those words. So of course when Mom needed care, Kira had stepped up, happily. Being the sole dependable caregiver to a totally dependent family member was not easy, Kira knew that firsthand. And she had little tolerance for family members unwilling to pitch in and help. "If you and your brothers are as concerned for your mother and father as you say you are, then maybe you all should spend less time threatening and complaining and trying to find someone else to do it, and actually go home and help."

Kira was out of line, she knew it. But she'd reached her limit.

Apparently so had Dr. Limone, because without further comment, he slammed the phone down in her ear. Maybe it was childish, but Kira slammed down her phone right back.

The door to her office opened slightly and Connie stuck her head in. "You okay?"

No. Kira was not okay. She didn't let clients rattle her. But this guy...and his brother and father...the absolute nerve! "I'm fine."

"Mr. Jeffries wants to see you in his office," Connie said quietly.

Mr. Jeffries. The CEO. Uh oh. "Did he say why?" Kira's chest tightened.

Connie shook her head, looking grim. They

both knew Mr. Jeffries never asked Kira to his office for anything good.

Kira strained to inhale, expanding her lungs to full capacity to make sure they were working as she glanced at the clock. Still not even noon and she was ready to call it a day. "When?"

"As soon as you're off the phone."

Kira stood.

"I spoke with Myra," Connie said. "She told me they don't have a Daisy Limone as a patient."

That didn't make any sense. "One more thing I'll have to look into." Kira made a note on her ever-growing To Do list.

"She said another certified home health care agency has been approved in her area. Wants to know why all of our patients are suddenly going to them?"

A very good question that Kira would find the answer to as soon as she could find a free minute.

"Do me another favor?" she asked Connie.

"Name it."

"Tonight, at the bar, please don't let me drink

too much." The way she felt right now, it was a definite possibility.

Connie gave her a "yeah, right" look. "You know, maybe if you let loose once in a while you wouldn't be wound so tight and grabbing for your chest every time Mr. Jeffries's name is mentioned."

Kira looked down at her hand resting on her sternum.

"What if tonight, *you* get rip-roaring drunk?" Connie said. "And I make sure *you* get home to my apartment safely?"

Kira shook her head. "I can't. I start administrative call at eight on Saturday morning." If her week was any indication, this weekend would likely be a nightmare. "I can't be hungover." She eyed Connie. "Sheila's the case manager on call."

"Well that sucks."

Exactly.

Sheila, who had been working at WCHC twice as long as Kira. Sheila, who had been considered for the position of Director of Case Management at the same as Kira. Sheila, who had not taken

Kira's promotion well and spent a good deal of time searching out evidence of why she believed Kira should not be the Director of Case Management, which she happily shared with Mr. Jeffries. Sheila, who just happened to be Daisy Limone's case manager.

# CHAPTER TWO

THIS HAD TO be the stupidest thing Dr. Derrick Limone had ever done. Considering all the crazy stuff he'd gotten himself into as a teenager that was saying something. An uncle in law enforcement had kept him out of jail. Pure dumb luck had kept him alive and in one piece.

But he'd moved past all that had gotten his life together. He was a respectable physician now, living a respectable, law-abiding life.

At least until tonight, when he'd followed Ms. Kira Peniglatt from her office to the very bar where he now sat…staring into a half empty mug of beer, contemplating the best way to snatch her away from her friend and calculating the possible consequences of doing so.

Desperation led people to do stupid things.

In the past, his stupidity could be blamed on

a desperate need for excitement to alleviate the mundane boredom of small-town life.

Tonight...tonight was payback, not that he could ever fully repay his parents for all they'd done for him. But today he'd planned to travel down to the New York City office of We Care Health Care to get a start on trying.

Only a walk-in patient complaining of chest pain had made him miss his train. And an insane amount of late Friday afternoon traffic had made him too late to catch her during business hours. So when he'd seen her leaving her office building, he'd followed her. Like a deranged stalker.

She laughed, a loud, confident, bold sound that caught his attention every single time, as if there weren't dozens of other people in the crowded bar. He glanced her way to see her tossing back a third shot of Southern Comfort with lime. Apparently she hadn't stopped by for a quick drink before heading home, as he'd hoped.

The professional portrait of Ms. Kira Peniglatt, MSN, MBA, CCM, RN, Director of Case Management, on the insurance company website, where she wore conservative business attire, trendy glasses, and had her dark hair pulled back off of her face, had made it easy for Derrick to identify her leaving work. It hadn't prepared him for the smiling, laughing beauty out of her stuffy suit jacket, with her long, wavy hair hanging loose around her shoulders and a silky white sleeveless blouse leaving her firm arms bare while hugging her appealing curves. Or that skirt, clinging to her narrow hips. Or her long, slender legs. Or those fashionable four-inch black, shiny heels.

Derrick looked away, shaking his head as he did, wondering if maybe she had a twin who worked with her and he'd followed the wrong Ms. Peniglatt. Because the very appealing woman seated two tables away did not in any way resemble the uncompromising, coldhearted female he'd spoken with on the phone that morning. The same woman who'd told him to get her a signed HIPPA form, and then, after he'd inconvenienced his uncle to drive out to his parents' house to get one signed and then fax it back to him, had not taken any of his afternoon phone calls.

"Coming down to the city was an asinine idea," Derrick mumbled to himself. Then he picked up his mug and gulped down the rest of his beer. Even if he could separate Ms. Peniglatt from her friend, after three shots of Southern Comfort and two glasses of white wine in under two hours, she'd be in no condition to talk business.

He glanced at his watch. Almost seven. If he left now he could grab a couple of slices of pizza and make it up to Mom and Dad's house before midnight. Ms. Peniglatt had been right. Family takes care of family. The least Derrick could do, in addition to getting the home care straightened out to make sure his mother received the maximum benefit allowed, was to head home for the weekend when his dad needed him. That had meant helping his overworked receptionist/medical biller to reschedule and refer his weekend patients so he could close his office on Saturday. And finding someone to cover on call for the whole weekend, which hadn't been easy.

Thinking of everything he'd done today and everything he still had to do if he wanted his new practice to be a success, exhausted him. So he stopped thinking about it. Slapping a ten dollar bill on the bar to cover his drink and a tip, Derrick stood, stretched out his sore back, and headed to the bathroom so he could hopefully make the drive without stopping.

After taking care of business, so to speak, he exited into the dimly lit hallway at the back of the bar, and walked right into… "I'm sorry." He grabbed a hold of the dark-haired woman he'd almost knocked over.

"Don't be. It's not you, it's me." She wobbled. "Or rather these heels." Leaning heavily on his arm, she reached down to adjust her shoe. "A few drinks and they've become a detriment to me and those around me." She looked up, hesitated as if trying to place his face then smiled. "Or maybe it's fate."

If so, then fate was a nasty bitch to finally give him Ms. Peniglatt's full attention, when he had a signed HIPPA form in his pocket…when she was drunk and of no use to him.

"I saw you watching me," she said.

Half the men in the bar and a good number of women were watching her. She was beautiful to look at. But Derrick knew firsthand that a total lack of compassion lurked beneath her unexpectedly appealing façade.

"Dare I take that to mean you like what you see?" She raised a pair of perfectly shaped eyebrows.

What heterosexual male wouldn't? God help him she smelled fantastic, classy, enticing.

"Are you mute?" she asked, scrunching her brow.

No, he was not mute. But like a dumbfounded idiot, he shook his head rather than responding verbally.

"I'm Kira," she introduced herself, pressing her body to his to make room in the hallway for two women to walk past, so close he could feel the swell of her breasts against his chest, the push of her hip against his… Damn. She felt even better than she smelled. His body hardened with interest, with…yearning. Not good. He tried to push her away.

But Ms. Peniglatt would have none of that. Surprisingly steady after all the liquor she'd consumed, she skillfully turned them, pinning his back to the wall. "And you are?"

"Derrick." His name came out coarse, like it was the first word he'd uttered in a decade, like he was a virgin who'd never been hit on by a beautiful woman before. Come to think of it, if he ever had, it'd been too long ago for him to remember. Between medical school, then residency and now working an insane amount of hours at his six-month-old private family practice, he didn't get out much. When he did, *he* liked to be the one to make the first move.

"Nice to meet you, Derrick." She leaned in to whisper in his ear. "Are you married, or engaged, or in a relationship?" Her hands slid up the sides of his dress shirt then back down to settle on his hips leaving a pleasing, fizzy feeling wherever she'd touched him.

He fought back a laugh. In all the possible outcomes he'd considered when first deciding to follow Ms. Peniglatt when he'd seen her hailing a cab outside of her office, he'd never once entertained the possibility she'd come on to him. Or that he'd have to fend her off or think of a way to politely turn her down, without letting her know his true identity.

"Because I've been watching you, too, Derrick," she said seductively. "And I very much like what *I* see. I've had a horrible, train wreck of a week. But at this very moment, things are looking up because here you are when I just happen to be drunk enough to pick up a total stranger in a bar."

He wasn't exactly a *total* stranger.

"So if you're interested…" She moved her mouth to his neck and set a gentle kiss just above his collar sending a flair of arousal through his system. "I'd very much like for the two of us to spend the rest of the night together." She moved her mouth back up to his ear and whispered, "Naked."

*Naked.* At the sound of the word, at the feel of her hot, moist breath as she said it and the enticing visual images that accompanied it, his body perked up in eager anticipation. Under normal circumstances, Derrick would like nothing more than to get naked with a woman as attractive and alluring as the woman pressed against him.

But there was nothing normal about the circumstances of their meeting.

"That feels nice," she said, setting her cheek to his shoulder.

What felt nice? Oops. Somehow his hands had wound up on her spectacular ass, which did, in fact, feel *very* nice. He couldn't help but give a little squeeze.

*Remember why you're here.*

He removed his hands. "I—"

"Well look at you." Kira's friend joined them. "I was wondering what was taking so long. Please tell me you know this man."

"We've just recently become acquainted," Kira said, pulling away guiltily, almost stumbling. Derrick reached out to steady her, and somehow she wound up right back where she'd started, pressed to his chest.

"Quick reflexes. Good thing. I'm Connie, Kira's assistant." She held out her hand.

Derrick shook it.

"She's also my best friend," Kira added, in a sappy drunk kind of way. "Although she's failed miserably in keeping me from getting drunk tonight."

"As your best friend," Connie said, "I consider it my responsibility to remind you that you're not the type to pick up strange men in bars." She looked up at Derrick. "You'll have to excuse her. She doesn't get out much."

"One night," Kira said sleepily, cuddling up against him. "My sister is home. I have a whole night to myself to have fun and do whatever I want and I want to spend it with Derrick."

Why did her sister need to be home for her to have a night all to herself?

"That's the alcohol talking," Connie said.

"I like what it's saying," Kira said back, looking up at Derrick. "Don't you like what it's saying, Derrick?"

He was going to hell, because for damn sure he most certainly did like what it was saying, what *she* was saying.

Connie looked conflicted. "You don't know anything about him," Connie said. Glancing up to meet his eyes she added, "No offense. I'm sure you're a great guy."

No. Tonight he wasn't. She felt so good, desire tried to overtake good moral character, screaming, "Take her to the nearest motel and give her what she wants, hard and fast. Exhaust her then leave while she's sleeping. She'll never know who you really are. First thing Monday morning, call her again like nothing happened." Common sense fought back, screaming, "You're not *that* guy. You don't take advantage of drunk women, no matter how sexy they are or how much you dislike them."

"You're the one who told me some hot sex would make me feel better," Kira said to Connie. "I've had a rotten day. I need to feel better." She wrapped her arms around his waist and squeezed. "Make me feel better, Derrick."

"She's not a big drinker," Connie explained apologetically.

All evidence to the contrary.

"Come on, Kira." Connie tugged on her arm. "Let the nice man be on his way."

Kira looked up at him, again, her expression soft and sweet. "Do you want to be on your way, Derrick?"

He *should* want to be on his way. He *needed* to be on his way, had a long drive ahead of him. And yet, "Not, really," snuck out of his mouth, followed by, "How about we go get a cup of coffee or something to eat?"

# CHAPTER THREE

KIRA CAME AWAKE to the smell of coffee. Oh, God. How did Mom get to the kitchen? She jumped out of bed and...

"Whoa," a man said. "Slow down."

She froze at the sound of a male voice in her bedroom. During that pause she noticed carpet below her bare feet. She didn't have carpet in her bedroom.

A quick perusal of her surroundings made her think she was in a child's room. One she didn't recognize. A single bed draped in a baseball-themed comforter, baseball trophies covering the desk and dresser, and posters of baseball players she didn't recognize hanging on the walls. Thumbtacks held a large periodic table on the back of the closed door. Funny, she'd done the same thing in her bedroom as a teenager, to hide her inner science geek.

But what the heck? She turned back to the handsome man before her, standing tall and solid, holding two mugs of coffee. He wore a tight white T-shirt that showcased a muscled chest and arms, and navy blue slacks. His feet were bare. Dark, mussed hair fell haphazardly over his forehead, and stuck up in spots. A day's worth of scruff covered his jaw. Kira liked scruff. But who was he? And why did his blue eyes stare back at her with a wary edge?

She studied the face, recognizing it. Derrick. Memories of last night whooshed into her mind, seeing him at the bar, watching him as he watched her, stumbling into him, pushing him against the wall, and oh, God, propositioning him. Connie taking a picture of him and his driver's license then patting him down for weapons before walking them out to his car to check that for weapons too. She shook her head in disbelief then dropped her forehead into her palm. "I'm sorry…

bad week. Too much to drink." Sexual depriva-tion. A night of freedom.

"So you said. Last night."

Kira could have done without the humor in his tone.

So what? She'd propositioned him. He was a good-looking guy. For sure she hadn't been the first. Embarrassment warmed her cheeks, be-cause there was a definite chance, a small one, but a chance nonetheless, that she could have been the first woman to refuse to get out of his car until he took her somewhere they could have sex. And she'd been pretty explicit about what she'd wanted.

Yet here she stood, fully dressed in the skirt and blouse she'd worn to work yesterday. "My clothes." She looked up at him. "We didn't…?"

He shook his head.

Well that sucked. The awkward morning after without the night of hot sex that should have pre-ceded it.

"Why not? Didn't you want to?"

Damn he had a nice smile. "Yeah, I wanted to. But it wouldn't have been right."

Wouldn't have been right? Why the hell not? Two consenting adults. Check. Mutual attraction. Hmmm. Had their attraction been mutual? The feel of his arousal, big and hard beneath her while she'd straddled him in the front seat of his car came to mind. Oh, yeah. Their attraction had been mutual. So why—?

Someone knocked on the closed bedroom door. Kira jumped.

"You want breakfast?" an older sounding male voice asked.

"We'll be down in a few minutes," Derrick said.

"Who was that?" Kira whispered, like whoever it was could hear her. Then she scanned the room for her shoes, messenger bag, and briefcase. Time to go.

"My dad."

She swung around to face him. "Are you kidding me? You live with your parents and you brought me home to their house?" At the age of thirty, Kira was way too old to be worried about getting caught in a boy's bedroom by his parents. Yet she found herself glancing toward the window as a means of escape.

"Second floor," Derrick said, as if he could read her mind.

But Kira was focused on what she saw outside that window...or rather what she didn't see. She stepped closer.

No big buildings, no crowded streets. No closely spaced buildings or brownstones or houses. No signs she was in New York City or any of its five boroughs. No, sirree. He'd taken her someplace rural, with lots of trees, wide open spaces, and no neighbors that she could see out of what appeared to be a back window. She squinted off into the distance. Heaven help her, was that a...cow?

Maybe fear would have been an appropriate response right then, but Kira got mad and turned on him. "Where the hell am I?"

"I can explain," he said, holding out a cup of coffee. "You're probably going to need this."

Kira eyed the dark liquid. Last night, alcohol had allowed a far-too-long-ignored desire for sex to overtake her usually strong protective instincts. Well, this morning they were back at fully functional. She didn't know this man, didn't know what he was capable of, and would most certainly not drink a beverage she had not watched him prepare, regardless of how much she wanted it.

"It's coffee," he said. "Do you want me to take a sip before you drink it?"

"I want you to explain what's going on." Seeing her shoes, bag and briefcase lined up neatly at the foot of the bed, she bent to pick them up. "Where am I, and why is your father here?"

"Fine." He set one mug of coffee down on the dresser. "If you change your mind, help yourself." He walked over to the small desk, pulled out an old wooden chair and sat down. "Sorry, but I need to sit. I've been up watching you most of the night and I'm exhausted." He took a sip of coffee.

"Watching me? That's not at all creepy." It was totally creepy. She took one step closer to the door.

"Wrong choice of words." He ran his fingers through his hair, pushing it out of his eyes. "I've been up most of the night waiting for you to wake up. So you didn't freak out. So I could explain..."

"Go ahead then. Explain." Kira sat on the corner of the bed closest to the door, making sure she had a clear path, her hand inside the bag on her lap, her fingers wrapped around the canister of pepper spray she kept on her keychain. Just in case.

"Remember how I told you it wouldn't have been right for me to have sex with you?"

She nodded.

"That's because my being in that bar last night wasn't a random coincidence." He looked her straight in the eyes. "I'd followed you from your office."

Kira didn't wait to hear more. "That's it." She stood. "I'm out of here."

Derrick stood, too.

The movement wasn't in any way threatening, but when he reached for her Kira whipped out the pepper spray and held it few inches from his face. "Don't."

He stopped and held up both hands in surrender. "I'm not going to hurt you."

"No, you're not," Kira told him, standing tall and on guard, confident in her ability to protect herself thanks to several self-defense classes. "By the way, I've been taught that you should never trust a man who says 'I'm not going to hurt you,' because that means he's thought about it."

"Or," Derrick countered, his hands still raised up by his shoulders, "it means he realizes he's bigger and stronger and he really doesn't want you to think he's going to use his size or strength to hurt you."

He said the words matter-of-factly, but Kira could sense his tension.

"Who are you? Why were you following me?"

"I'm Derrick Limone."

Limone. Why did that name sound familiar?

"I got a HIPPA form signed and faxed it down to your office, just like you asked. Then you wouldn't take my phone calls. So late yesterday

afternoon I rushed down to the city to meet you
at your office to give it to you in person so you'd
speak with me about my mother."

His mother. "Daisy Limone." Un-friggin'-be-
lievable.

"I missed my train," he went on. "So I drove
down from White Plains, in Westchester County,
where I live and work. I drove past your office
just as you and Connie were getting into a cab
out front...so I followed it."

"You followed it? You think that's acceptable
behavior to follow me after business hours? Why
on earth would you do such a thing?" Because
he was a total nut job!

"You wouldn't take my calls."

He said it like it made perfect sense. It didn't.
The man was obviously not right in the head.
"Which son are you?" she asked. "The attorney
who called me degrading names and threatened
to sue me or the doctor who yelled at me and
hung up on me?"

"The doctor," he admitted, looking guilty. "But

in my defense, you were giving me a pretty hard time."

Not as hard as he deserved for not stepping up to take care of his mother like a good son should. *His mother.* Then it clicked. Him taking Kira to a rural location, his father knocking on the door. Her eyes went wide and she sucked in a breath. He didn't! "I'm at your parents' house? In West Guilderford?" Four hours from her home.

He just stood there.

"You really are insane." She backed toward the door. "As in mentally unhinged and in need of inpatient psychiatric therapy. Immediately."

"No. I'm not."

"You kidnapped me!"

"Kidnapped you?" He crossed his arms over his chest. "Let's talk about that, shall we?"

He seemed way too calm for a man on the verge of being arrested. *Because he's insane! Run while you can!*

Kira lunged for the doorknob.

Showing amazing speed and agility, Derrick lunged too, grabbing the pepper spray and putting his full weight against the door to keep it closed. "Not so fast," he said, looking down at her while keeping his shoulder pressed to the door. "You are not leaving this room thinking I kidnapped you."

"Let's look at the facts, shall we?" Kira held up her right index finger. "One. You followed me out to the bar last night. Two." She added her middle finger. Hmmm. How to tactfully put it? "You lured me out of that bar under false pretenses."

He actually had the nerve to laugh. "I did not *lure* you anywhere. I offered to take you for coffee and something to eat—"

"We both know you only said that to appease Connie." Kira waved him off. "I offered you sex and you accepted my offer without ever intending to follow through."

"No. I offered you coffee and something to eat and I had fully intended to follow through with *that*, but you refused to get out of the car when we got to the diner."

"Because I wanted..."

"You wanted what?"

Sex, damn it. She'd wanted sex not coffee and not something to eat.

Based on his slow, sexy smile, he knew exactly what she'd wanted.

That, and the fact he hadn't given it to her, pissed her off. So she pushed his chest. "Go to hell."

"Help me out here," he said. "Are you mad because you think I kidnapped you or because we didn't have sex?"

Both! "You're an ass."

"Maybe," he said. "But I'm not a kidnapper."

"Then how, exactly, did I wind up here at your parents' house, with no recollection of how I got here? I don't recall you asking. And I don't recall agreeing to come."

"That can easily be explained by the amount of alcohol you drank last night." With a tilted head and raised eyebrows he simply said, "You passed out."

No. Kira shook her head. No way. She had never in her life consumed enough alcohol to pass out. "Fell asleep, maybe. But I most certainly did not pass out. Okay, let's say you're telling the truth and I *fell asleep* in your car."

"I *am* telling the truth," he said confidently, still blocking her escape.

"So there I am, asleep in your car, and all you can think to do is take me on the four hour drive up to your parents' house?"

"What would you have liked me to do with you?" he challenged.

"Oh, I don't know. Maybe take me to my home?" she yelled.

"You have no memory of what happened after we got to the restaurant, do you?"

No, not really.

"You don't remember me going through your bag to find your wallet to find your driver's license?"

Nope. "If I had seen you doing that I would have told you I don't have a driver's license." She'd lived in New York City all her life and couldn't afford to keep a car, so she'd never bothered to learn how to drive.

"I found a few college IDs, a bunch of credit

cards, and insurance cards. But you know what I didn't find?" He didn't give her a chance to answer. "Anything with your current address on it."

Very possible.

"So I tried your phone, hoping I could find a home number or Connie's number."

She winced. "You need a security code to access it."

"Yes, you do." He shifted his position so his back rested against the door. "And even though I could rouse you to ask, you weren't giving up the code, any phone numbers, or your address. So there I sat, parked on Thirty-Eighth Street with a drunk woman fast asleep in my front seat."

"You could have tried harder to wake me up."

"Oh, I tried," he said. "For the record, you are very cranky when your sleep is disturbed."

That was true.

"So there I sat," he repeated. "A drunk woman fast asleep in my front seat. No idea where she lived and unable to contact anyone on her phone while the minutes ticked by. I sat there for an hour, Kira. Then I tried to wake you again. You grumbled and complained in words I couldn't understand. I asked where you lived. You refused to tell me. But you know what you did say, loud and clear?"

Kira wasn't sure she wanted to know.

Too bad, because Derrick seemed intent on telling her. "You said, 'Take me home with you. I want to go home with you.' Over and over. So you know what? That's exactly what I did. I brought you home with me."

Kira narrowed her eyes. "I don't believe you."

He reached into the front pocket of his slacks and pulled out his cell phone, pressed a few buttons, then held out the screen for her to watch and listen to him trying to get her home address and her refusing to answer.

"You took a video of me?" And not a very flattering one. Yikes!

He nodded. "You seemed like the kind of woman who'd want proof."

That she was. She'd glanced away from the screen but looked back in time to see and hear herself say, "I want to go home with you. Take me home with you."

Kira turned to face the window. "I'm never drinking alcohol out in public again."

Derrick walked up behind her. For some strange reason she didn't feel at all threatened by his closeness. "I didn't go down to the city planning to bring you up here. But I'd had every intention of heading up after I met with you. Family takes care of family. You were right. So I cleared my appointment schedule and got someone to cover for me so I could help my dad this weekend. I didn't know what else to do with you. It was getting late. My dad was depending on me to be here this morning. So I brought you with me. As soon as I spend some time with my parents and help get Mom settled for the day, I'll take you home."

Kira turned to face him. "Thank you."

"Now let's go down and have some breakfast, then you can meet Mom, last I checked, she was still sleeping."

Go down and have breakfast, as in with his

father? Kira would rather starve. "Your father hates me."

Derrick smiled. "He doesn't hate you. As far as he knows you're my friend Kira who wanted to come home with me this weekend."

"*Wanted?* That's a bit of a stretch, don't you think?"

"We can go downstairs and tell him the truth if you want." Derrick headed for the door. "Your call."

"Wait. No." Kira followed him. "Let's not."

# CHAPTER FOUR

"WHERE'S YOUR FRIEND?" Dad asked when Derrick entered the kitchen.

He looked old and worn-out in his standard at-home summer attire, a dingy white tank undershirt, his navy blue heavy-duty mechanic uniform pants cut off at the knee—because why waste money on shorts when you could cut up old pants?—and his black, steel toe work shoes with white socks.

"She freshening up," Derrick answered, pulling out a chair and sitting down at one of the spots Dad had set at the kitchen table. "You didn't have to go to all this trouble." Mom's sunny yellow tablecloth with matching placemats and napkins dressed up the usually bare round wooden table. And he'd put out the floral glasses Mom saved for company—because heaven forbid her rambunctious sons should break them.

"This is the first girl you've brought home since high school. It's a big deal."

Kira Peniglatt was hardly a girl. She was a full grown, much too appealing woman. "She's just a friend," he lied. Hopefully she could remain civil through breakfast and until they left. He'd have to figure out a way to break it to his mom and dad that he wouldn't be staying through Sunday as planned.

Derrick eyed the offerings on the table. Fresh croissants and Danish. Butter and a jar of Mom's homemade raspberry preserves. A fruit bowl filled with fresh peaches, plums and bananas. Dad set a casserole dish on a trivet in the center of the table. It contained scrambled eggs and bacon he'd taken from the oven where apparently he'd been keeping it hot. "Pop. You went all out. When did you have time—?"

"I asked Mrs. Holmes to run out to the store for me this morning," Dad said. Their neighbor of more than forty years was also Mom's best friend. "If your mama could, she would have done it. But she can't." Dad turned away to put the oven mitts on the counter and grab a serving spoon.

The sadness in his dad's voice squeezed Derrick's heart. His first instinct was to say something like, "She'll be back to shopping on her own in no time." But it was too early in her recovery to know that for sure. Derrick didn't want to give his dad false hope.

"Well hello, there," Dad said, surprisingly cheerful all of a sudden.

"Good morning, Mr. Limone," Derrick heard Kira say.

He stiffened. Things this morning had gone much better than he'd hoped. But how would she act toward his father? Would she keep her identity and how she'd wound up here secret?

"Thank you so much for having me on such short notice," she said, her pleasant almost friendly tone a surprise.

He relaxed then turned in his chair. She'd changed into skin tight leggings that stopped at her knees and a clingy pale pink tank top with straps too skinny to cover those from her purple bra. When she saw him looking she shrugged as if to say, "It's all I had with me. Deal with it." From the heterosexual male point of view she looked fantastic. Plus now he wouldn't have to explain why she didn't have a change of clothes with her. A win-win.

She'd washed off the mascara that'd smudged around her eyes in the night, so pretty, even without makeup. Her hair was set in a loose braid draped over her right shoulder. She looked so much softer and more approachable than her ultra-serious professional business portrait on the website. Who was the real Kira?

"Come," Dad said, motioning to the table with a spatula. "Sit down and eat before it gets cold."

"Wow." Kira took the chair across from him. "This looks delicious."

"I was hoping you weren't one of those 'just coffee for breakfast' types." Dad sat down between them. "Dig in." He handed the spatula to Kira. "Don't be shy."

Derrick watched as she served herself a small helping of eggs and one strip of bacon, wondering if she *was* one of those 'just coffee for breakfast' types. Speaking of which. "Can I pour you a cup of coffee? From the pot both my dad and I are drinking out of?" He added that last part because it was obvious she didn't trust him. Really, why should she?

"I'd love a cup." She offered him a sweet albeit fake smile. "With a splash of milk from the same container you and your father are using," she added, giving it right back to him. He kind of liked that.

"Well, I gotta hand it to you, boy," Dad said. "Whatever you said to that evil Peniglatt woman at the insurance company, really worked."

Derrick swung around and cautioned, "Dad. Kira doesn't want to hear about your problems with the insurance company."

The topic of discussion, who sat ramrod straight at the moment, placed her napkin in her lap somewhat stiffly. "On the contrary," she said, looking straight at him in challenge. "I'd like to hear whatever your dad has to say."

Why had he traveled down to the city yesterday? Why had he brought Kira home with him? Why? Why? Why? Derrick hurried back to the table, determined to change the subject.

"My wife, Daisy, had a stroke, you see," Dad said as he loaded his plate with eggs and bacon.

"How is Mom doing this morning," Derrick asked. "Last I checked she was sleeping."

"I walked her to the bathroom earlier." Dad looked at Kira. "She's weak and gets real tired real easy. So she went back to sleep after. Which reminds me." He turned his head to Derrick. "We're getting a shipment of medical equipment this morning. So eat up quick. We may have to move some furniture around."

"Medical equipment?" Derrick asked Kira.

But Dad answered. "Like I was saying, after you let that insurance company witch have it, she got right on the ball and sent out a new nurse from a different agency to visit your mama late yesterday afternoon. A real good one. Stayed for over an hour."

Derrick looked at Kira.

"You must have given it to her but good," she said, staring straight at Derrick as she leaned back in her chair and crossed her arms over her chest.

"It's him being a doctor," Dad said around a mouthful of eggs. "Them insurance company types stand up and listen when a doctor starts talking."

"That must have been it." Kira shifted in her seat, reaching for her glass to take a sip of orange juice. "She couldn't possibly have investigated the situation, identified a problem and fixed it." She leaned in Derrick's direction. "You're a hero." Her words dripped with sarcasm...which apparently his dad missed.

"Yes he is," Dad said proudly. "Took on that heartless beast and won."

Derrick wanted to crawl under the table and become one with the floorboards.

If a stare could actually burn a hole in some-

one's head, Derrick would have one right between the eyes, courtesy of Miss Kira Peniglatt.

"Dad—" Derrick started, prepared to explain
everything.

"Don't you 'Dad' me." Dad turned to Kira.
"He is a hero. He saves lives. Lots of 'em. He's
a good man who knows how to treat a woman
right. Taught him how myself, I did." Dad actually puffed out his chest. Then he pointed at Kira
with his fork. "He's a good catch. Any woman
would be lucky to have him."

"So lucky," Kira repeated with a smirk.

Derrick lost his appetite. "Stop it, Dad. I don't
need a matchmaker." All he needed was to survive this morning without Dad finding out Kira's
true identity, tolerate her long enough to get her
home safely, and then get back to his normal, uneventful life, where he was in control of things…
at least where he used to be in control of things.

When someone knocked on the door, Derrick
jumped up to answer, happy beyond belief to escape the breakfast table.

The next two hours flew by in a whirl of activity as two deliverymen from the durable medical equipment company showed up. Kira took control, ordering around four grown men with the effectiveness of a five star general. No one dared question her.

The woman was a sight to behold, in her element, knowledgeable, efficient and concise. Damn he needed someone like her in his office someone to take charge and get things running smoothly.

"She's really something," Dad said, blotting his brow with his ever present cotton handkerchief.

"Yes she is." Derrick watched her take on a man who outweighed her by at least two hundred pounds, refusing to accept a wheelchair because one of the wheel brakes didn't work to her satisfaction. "We need a replacement before the end of the day," she said.

"Sure thing, Kira," the man said, respect evident in his tone.

"I'll be calling Al on Monday to let him know how hard you both worked today and how accommodating you were." With a twenty dollar incentive for each of them, the deliverymen helped Derrick move the couches, a bed, a TV stand plus TV, and an old shelving unit packed with knickknacks so his father didn't have to do any heavy lifting. And Kira had gotten right in there to help, boxing up papers, sweeping up dust from the old wood floors after the furniture was moved, and making up the big hospital bed now sitting in the living room.

"Who's Al?" Dad asked.

"I have no idea."

"You didn't tell me she was a nurse."

A damn good one at that, an amazing one, actually. When Dad balked about them putting the hospital bed in the living room rather than in an upstairs bedroom, Kira spoke calmly and convincingly, warning him of the safety hazard of having Mom in an upstairs bedroom when she couldn't walk or manage stairs on her own. How would he get her out of the house if there was a fire? She pointed out having Mom on the main level of the house would mean less trips up and down the stairs to alleviate Dad's knee and hip discomfort. Derrick didn't even know Dad was having knee and hip discomfort.

When Dad groused about him and Mom having to sleep in separate beds in separate rooms Kira reminded him that it wasn't forever, then she demonstrated the benefits of raising and lowering an electronic bed to help alleviate the strain on Dad's back when he cared for Mom. She pointed out the positives of a more stimulating environment where Mom could watch television, visit with friends, and be with Dad while he performed his daily activities rather than being hidden away in a lonely bedroom for hours at a time. And she suggested moving one of the twin beds from upstairs down to the living room so Mom and Dad could sleep together, in the same room at least.

Dad balked at a wheelchair. He wanted his wife up and walking around so she could get stronger. Kira told him to only use the wheelchair when he could tell Mom was tired. To help her get to the small bathroom off the kitchen or out to the porch for some fresh air.

The woman was a master.

"I got an aide coming on Monday," Dad said. "Three hours a day, five days a week. She's mostly to help with exercises and therapy stuff, but the home care nurse said while she's here the aide can help your mom learn to bathe and dress herself."

"Why didn't you tell me any of this yesterday?" It would have saved Derrick a lot of time and effort.

"Didn't want to bother you at work, I figured I'd tell you when you got here."

Kira closed the door behind the deliverymen and handed Dad some paperwork. "They'll be back at some point this afternoon with a new wheelchair. The raised toilet seat has been installed in the bathroom off of the kitchen, but can be moved at any time. The commode chair by the bed is only for emergencies. There's a tub chair in the bathroom down here so Daisy can wash up at the sink. It can also be used in the tub upstairs when she gets a more thorough bath or is ready to start showering. You own all three of them. There's a sticker on the footboard of the bed. When you no longer need the wheelchair and hospital bed, just call the number and the company will return to pick them up."

"I could hug you," Dad told Kira.

"Go ahead." She held open her arms and smiled.

"Thank you," he said, hugging her tightly. "Thank you, so…much."

Over Dad's shoulder Kira's eyes met his before she quickly looked away. "You're very welcome. But it's not me you should be thanking. Miss Peniglatt got you what you need. Maybe you should give her a call to thank *her.*"

"No way in hell," Dad said, stepping back. "She only done it because Derrick made her."

Not true.

"Bet it made her good and mad, too." Dad smiled. "Wish I could have been there to see it."

Derrick needed to come clean, to tell his dad the truth. But just as he was about to, a bell rang from upstairs. Dad's face brightened. "Your mama's awake." With the sole focus of getting to her, he immediately turned his back on both of them and headed for the stairs.

Kira stood there looking unsure of what to do. "See. I told you, he hates me."

"He may dislike Miss Peniglatt from We Care Health Care." Hate was such a strong word. "But he adores Kira the nurse who has been such a big help today. I can't thank you enough."

"We're the same person." Kira ignored his thanks, seeming truly bothered by what his father thought of her.

"But he doesn't know you're the same person." Not yet, anyway. At some point Derrick would tell him. Just not with her present. Dad could be...unpredictable at times. "Come upstairs and meet my mom."

Kira shook her head. "I don't think that's such a good idea. She probably hates me, too."

"Mom loves everyone. Come on." He held out his hand.

Kira stepped back.

"Do you ever visit any of the patients who

receive case management services from your company?"

"I worked as a community health nurse for a year and a half before taking a job as a case manager at WCHC. I've visited plenty of patients in their homes."

"That must have been a lot of years ago. Have you visited any since? As the Director of Case Management, out in the field, following up to see how WCHC patients are faring with the services and equipment authorized?"

Kira shook her head. "Never had the time...or the opportunity."

"Well today you do."

Kira didn't respond. He had no intention of forcing her. "Hang out down here, if you like. Dad has basic cable on the TV. Remote's on the arm of his recliner." Derrick pointed. "Shower if you want."

She gave him a look that had him holding up both hands and saying, "Not that you smell or anything." Jeez. "But later on this afternoon I'd like to take you to a nice lunch." Well, as nice as they could get in these parts. "To show my appreciation for all you've done and as an apology. I misjudged you."

"There's no need to take me out to eat as a thank you for doing my job. Your mom was eligible for everything I authorized. I apologize for the fact it was not offered or recommended by the first home health care nurse to visit." Her eyes met his. "And why is it all you want to do when you're with me is eat and drink coffee?" She looked down her body. "Am I too skinny?"

Slender, yes, appealingly so. But Kira had curves in all the places he liked them. "For your information," he stared down into her eyes. "I can recall, in vivid, most enjoyable detail, the feel of your stunning body pressed up against mine last night." He lowered his voice and leaned in close to her when he added, "And straddling my lap in the car."

Kira's cheeks went pink but she maintained eye contact. Good for her.

"Trust me when I tell you," he went on. "Eating and drinking coffee are not the *only* things

I want to do with you." He gave her a look to let her know exactly what he was thinking.

"Yes, well." Rather than meet his eyes she looked down, wiping some dust from her left thigh. "Now that I know who you really are, *that's* not going to happen."

"Why not?" he asked, even though he already knew the answer.

She looked straight at him. "Because you're the family member of a patient receiving case management services from a member of my staff. It's a conflict of interest and would be highly unprofessional."

Yes to both. Yet he couldn't let it drop. "But you want to," he said, watching her, needing to know for certain that her attraction to him last night was not solely the result of alcohol lowering her inhibitions.

She glanced away...hesitated...a surefire affirmative response as far as he was concerned. Yes! But before he could do anything about it, Dad called down, "Don't keep your mother waiting. She wants to see you."

"We're coming," Kira called back, hurrying toward the stairs.

Derrick watched the sway of her hips and the movement of her tight, round, sexy ass.

"Those pants, on a woman with your figure, should be illegal."

She glanced back at him with a sexy grin then took the stairs two at a time.

# CHAPTER FIVE

KIRA FOLLOWED THE sound of Mr. Limone's voice to a bedroom at the end of the hallway, stopping in the doorway at the sight of him sitting on his wife's side of their full-sized bed, leaning down to kiss her on the forehead, carefully, lovingly. Kira's heart squeezed as she remembered her dad kissing her mom like that, years ago, after making her breakfast in bed for her birthday, a few months before he'd issued his ultimatum and then walked out when he didn't like Mom's choice. Back when Kira used to dream about someday finding a man who loved her as much as Dad loved Mom. Back when she'd believed in happily-ever-after and until-death-do-us-part.

"Still in love after fifty-four years of marriage," Derrick said quietly from behind her.

It was truly a beautiful scene.

Mr. Limone noticed them. "Come in." He stood. "Meet Daisy." He motioned to his wife.

Derrick skirted around her and entered the room.

Upon seeing him Daisy gave a lopsided smile due to a right-sided facial droop from her stroke, most likely. Then she started to cry.

"Don't cry, Mom," Derrick said, hurrying to the bed.

Daisy reached up to hug him with her left arm. Kira noticed she tried to lift her right arm too, but that was the side affected by the stroke so the arm barely made if off the bed and it swayed awkwardly.

Derrick dropped to his knees by the side of the bed and Daisy hugged her son tightly with her good arm. "L-l-love," she said. "Love. Love."

"I love you, too, Mom."

Kira could hear the love in both of their voices. While she told her mother she loved her often, Kira couldn't remember the last time she'd said it back. They both had lost so much as a result of the attack.

"There's someone I want you to meet," Derrick said, bringing Kira's attention back to her present location.

She approached the bed. "Good morning, Mrs. Limone," she said formally, reaching down to squeeze her left hand. "So nice to meet you."

Daisy's eyes shifted from Kira to Derrick then back to Kira. "Day," she said, looking frustrated. "Dayyyy."

"She wants you to call her Daisy," Mr. Limone said, as if Kira couldn't figure that out. But she liked that he jumped in to help his wife communicate, although he'd have to stop doing that and let Daisy struggle to get the words out if he wanted her speech to improve. The therapist would go over that with him.

"Nice to meet you, Daisy." Kira tried to pull her hand back but Daisy held on tightly, her eyes once again moving from Kira to Derrick, back to Kira then back to Derrick, as if wondering what was going on between the two of them. "I'm a friend," Kira said, using the loosest definition of the word. "Just a friend."

Even without full movement of her facial musculature, Kira could read the disappointment on Daisy's face.

Derrick stood up. "Since I'm here, I'll be the one helping you get washed and dressed this morning."

Daisy released Kira, moved her hand with amazing speed, and jerked the bed covers up to her neck. "Noooo," she said loudly and succinctly.

Expressive aphasia aside, Daisy Limone made her opinions known.

"Please, Mom," Derrick tried to argue. "I want to help."

But Daisy wouldn't budge. "No." She made an angry face. "Noooooooooo."

Mr. Limone let out a weary, exhausted breath. "It's okay. I'll do it."

He looked drained. So Kira decided to offer up her services. Dropping to her knees beside the bed she said, "In addition to being a friend of your son's, I'm also a nurse." Daisy watched her quietly. "I have lots of experience helping women get washed up and dressed. If it's okay with you, I'm happy to help you today."

"That's not necessary," Derrick said. "I *want* to do it."

As a nurse, Kira understood both sides. She stood and turned to Derrick, speaking quietly. "I know you do. But there are some things a mother doesn't want her son to see."

Derrick nodded in understanding.

Kira turned back to the bed. "Your husband has been working hard since you came home."

Daisy's eye filled with tears as she nodded.

"He deserves a day off, don't you think?"

Daisy glanced at her husband with love, then turned back to Kira and nodded.

"I'm happy to help if you'll let me."

Daisy reached for Kira's hand and squeezed. "Love," she said.

Kira understood that was her way of expressing appreciation. "You're welcome."

The next hour spent with Daisy, helping her to wash up at the sink, washing her hair, then putting on some lipstick after she'd helped her dress, reminded Kira of why she'd become a nurse. To help people and to make a difference in their lives. As much as it pained her to admit it, after years of doing it day in and day out, caring for Mom felt like a chore. She didn't appreciate all that Kira did, her condition would never improve unless by some miracle of medicine the effects of a severe brain injury could be reversed.

"What do you think?" Kira stood behind Daisy, supporting her with the gait belt around her waist, as she looked in the full length mirror behind the door.

"Love," Daisy said, looking at herself with joy. Then her gaze shifted to Kira's and her expression changed. "Love," Daisy said, starting to tear up.

"You're very welcome. Now let's get you—"

Someone knocked on the door.

Kira helped Daisy move back. "Come in."

Derrick started to walk in then stopped in his tracks the look on his face making her wet clothing and sore back totally worth it. "What do you think?"

"I think…" He swallowed. "I think you look beautiful, Mom. Like the stroke never happened."

But the stroke had happened.

Daisy reached up to cup his cheek with her left hand.

"She's tired," Kira said to Derrick. "Daisy, do you want Derrick to carry you downstairs now or would you rather nap up here?"

Daisy took an eager step toward Derrick. He reached out to steady her.

Kira smiled. "Well, all righty then."

"Hold on. I need to talk to Kira for a minute. Grab that chair," he pointed to a wooden armchair in the corner of the room that had a bunch of male clothing draped over it. "Just throw those on the bed."

Kira did just that.

With Daisy seated, and propped with a pillow to keep her in place, Kira joined Derrick in the hallway.

"The sheriff's at the door asking to see you."

"Me?" Kira pushed some loose hairs off of her face and behind her ear. "Why?"

"He wouldn't say." Derrick looked at her accusingly.

"Well I didn't call him."

Why would the sheriff come here looking for her? Kira wondered as she hurried down the hallway and down the stairs. No one knew where she was. Seeing no one in the living room or kitchen, Kira hurried outside, where Derrick's dad stood, talking with the sheriff—a very large, very serious, very imposing man in full uniform—at the base of the porch steps. When he spotted her he asked, "Are you Kira Peniglatt?"

"Yes, officer," she answered as Mr. Limone shook his head unhappily, turned, and walked back into the house without sparing her a glance. Well she couldn't worry about him right now. "Is there a problem?"

"You tell me," he answered, studying her. "My office received a panicked phone call from a woman named," he pulled a pad out of his breast pocket and flipped to a page, "Connie, who's worried you were kidnapped and you're being held here against your will."

Kira smiled. Gotta love Connie. "I'm fine, Officer."

He looked over Kira's shoulder. She turned to see Derrick standing on the porch.

"So you weren't kidnapped?" the sheriff asked.

"No. I wasn't kidnapped." Not technically. "If Connie was worried, why didn't she just call my cell?" Kira pulled it out of the waistband of her leggings to check the screen. Almost fully charged. No messages.

"That's not going to do you any good around here," the sheriff said.

What? "Why not?"

Derrick came to stand beside her. "No cell service," he said matter-of-factly.

Wait. "What?" Kira's chest went tight and her heart started to pound. No, no, no. Her hand drifted up to her sternum. "No cell service?" She looked at the phone again. Closer this time. "That can't be. This is New York State. Everyone has cell service." But it could, in fact, be. And it was.

Kira's throat felt clogged with something big and uncomfortable.

"Welcome to the north country," Derrick said. "Hey." He bent to catch her gaze. "No worries. Use the phone in the kitchen to call her."

"No worries?" she asked, panic rising, pressure building in her head. "No worries?!" she yelled. "I'm on call this weekend. Being out of the city is no big deal, but I am required to be accessible by phone."

"On call? Why didn't you tell me?" Derrick asked.

"Why should I have to tell you? I charged my phone in your bedroom while we ate breakfast. I've been carrying it around with me all morning." She looked at the screen again. This could not be happening, not now, not after Mr. Jeffries had put her on probation yesterday afternoon.

"If you would have told me I would have told you we don't get cell service in this area."

The sheriff offered, "Some people can get a signal over in the library parking lot."

A lot of good that did Kira. "I need to make a call." She turned and ran up the porch steps.

"Your friend's waiting. Said to call her first," the sheriff called out. "Some big problem with one of your patients at work."

Of course there was. Of course the one weekend Kira didn't have cell service there would be a problem with one of her patients. When she reached the porch she stopped long enough to glance back and say, "Thank you for coming out, Sheriff. I'm sorry to have wasted your time. As you can see, I'm fine." Except for the fact she'd likely be unemployed come Monday. Mr. Jeffries had been looking for a reason to fire her for months. Unbeknownst to her, she'd just given him one.

Back inside the house Kira ran to the kitchen.

"Everything okay, *Miz Peniglatt*?" Derrick's dad asked.

Kira did not like his tone and she stopped long enough to tell him so. "Look, if you have a problem with my being here, take it up with your son. I assure you, while I am here of my own free will…now," she glared at Derrick who'd followed her in, "it was not my idea to bring me up here, and had I been included in the decision making, I would not have come. Now, I need to use your phone." She turned, added, "Please," and hurried into the kitchen, picked up the black wall-mounted phone and dialed Connie's cell phone number from memory.

She answered on the first ring. "Did you find her? Is she okay? Did you arrest that scum-sucking sonofabitch and throw him in jail?"

"I'm fine," Kira said, smiling. Only Connie could get her to smile at a time like this.

"Kira!" Connie screamed. "It's you! Oh, thank God, it's you! And you're fine! I have been scared out of my mind! When I couldn't find you on my Find My Friends App this morning I figured no biggie. You were probably too busy having spectacular sex to charge your phone last night, which hey, yay for you. But how would you do on call with a dead phone? So I figured maybe you'd gone home and were using your landline."

"Please tell me you didn't call my sister." This was getting worse by the second.

"What did you expect me to do? My best friend left the bar with a man neither of us knew, at least at the time I didn't know I knew him. Well, kind of knew him. When I couldn't reach you on your cell phone, I brought up the picture I took of Derrick's driver's license to get his address so I could look up his home phone number. That's when I recognized his full name. Do you know who he is?"

"Yes."

"No friggin' way! Did you know who he was last night when you were hanging all over him?"

*Don't remind me.* "No. He told me this morning. How did you figure out he brought me up to his parents' house?"

"Uh..."

"What?"

"I didn't know for sure so I sent police to his home address in White Plains first."

"You didn't."

"Sure did. His old neighbor said he didn't live

there anymore but he'd talked to Derrick and he'd mentioned visiting his parents this weekend. So I logged into your work computer remotely to get Daisy Limone's address."

"Connie! You're not supposed to have that log in!"

"Well I do." Kira could almost see the stubborn look on her assistant's face. "A good assistant needs to be prepared for anything."

Couldn't argue with that logic. Kira let out a breath. "Thank you for tracking me down."

"So," Connie said. "Did you...?"

"No. You need to call my sister and tell her you found me and I'm okay."

"No? All this trouble and you didn't—"

"No."

"Well, damn."

Yeah.

"Did you hear me?" Kira asked.

"Yes I heard you. But honestly, Krissy didn't sound all that worried. Said something like, "Kira can take care of herself," that was it."

Sounded like Krissy. She didn't worry about

much, mostly because Kira took care of herself and everything having to do with their mother which allowed Krissy to live the carefree life she'd enjoyed since they were kids, only worrying about herself. Maybe she should tell Connie not to call Krissy, leave her to wonder, give her the opportunity to picture life without Kira in it.

"What's going on at work?" Kira asked.

Talkative Connie stayed quiet.

Not good. "Tell me."

"Sheila freaked when she found out you reassigned Daisy Limone to another case manager."

Kira squeezed the bridge of her nose. She'd hoped she could wait until Monday to deal with that. "How did she find out?"

"The agency she'd referred the case to initially left a message that you'd taken back the referral."

"There's something shady going on there, Con." Kira planned to get to work very early on Monday morning to review all of Sheila's cases.

"I don't doubt it."

"Is there really a problem with one of our patients or is Sheila just making trouble?"

"I don't know. For whatever reason, she said she's been trying to get in touch with you and couldn't reach you. So of course she called—"

"Mr. Jeffries," Kira finished, the mere mention of the man's name causing a twinge of discomfort in her chest.

"Her boyfriend."

"We don't know that for certain." But most everyone in the office suspected. If the last CEO, the one who'd promoted Kira, hadn't been in his seventies and happily married, Sheila would have probably tried to seduce him for a promotion, too. She was just that type of person.

"How do you think she knows how to get in touch with him outside of work?" Connie asked. "Do all the case managers have his private phone number?"

No. They didn't. "How did you find out what's going on?"

"Mr. Jeffries called Alison to cover your on call for the rest of the weekend. She called me to see if everything was okay."

Alison, the Director of Utilization Review, a

nice enough woman, but rigid and by the book. Also a nurse, she and Kira split administrative night and weekend call duty. Since Alison had a husband and two young children, the split was around Kira: eighty percent of the time and Alison: the leftover twenty percent, which wasn't such a big deal because usually on call duty was very quiet, more of a formality than a necessity.

Kira leaned her shoulder against the wall and twisted the curly black phone cord around her fingers. "This is bad."

"Yup."

"Sorry."

"For what?"

"For making you worry," Kira said. "For giving Mr. Jeffries a reason to fire me so he can finally promote Sheila, which means come next week you'll likely be working for her."

"No way in hell that is going to happen. I'll quit."

Connie needed her job just as much as Kira did. "Let's not get ahead of ourselves. Maybe it's not as bad as it seems."

"Right," Connie said, trying to sound positive, unconvincingly so. "He can't fire you for one mistake."

No, technically he couldn't. But according to Mr. Jeffries, she'd been making lots of 'mistakes' lately. In his mind a 'mistake' consisted of any course of action he did not agree with. And he'd been sure to document each infraction. Forget the fact he wasn't a registered nurse and had no training in case management. "I'm going to have to call him."

"Or," Connie countered. "I won't tell anyone I tracked you down and you can show up to work Monday morning like nothing happened. What? You couldn't reach me? Why in the world not? I had my cell phone with me the whole time."

Kira smiled again. "Nice try."

"Waiting might give him a chance to cool down."

Probably not. "You really believe that?"

Connie didn't answer right away. "Look, he's going to yell at you either way, so why not enjoy a weekend completely off duty and deal with all this on Monday?" Connie said. "I have this number in my phone now in case I need you. When are you coming home?"

Kira glanced into the living room to see Derrick standing by Daisy's hospital bed, holding her hand, talking quietly. He was so gentle with her, so caring, such a good son. Kira felt kind of bad for being so hard on him.

"Probably tonight." Although with Krissy home and on call no longer her responsibility, Kira saw no reason to rush. Seeing how much Derrick's mom and dad were enjoying his company, she hated to be the reason he cut his visit short. "Maybe tomorrow." If she could find a local motel, since Mr. Limone would likely kick her out of the house now that he knew who she was. And if Krissy was willing to stay with Mom, two days in a row was asking a lot. "Don't bother calling Krissy. I'll give her a call now."

Then she'd call Mr. Jeffries.

# CHAPTER SIX

AFTER HER CONVERSATION with Connie, Kira called her sister, Krissy.

Derrick tried not to eavesdrop, really he did. But Mom and Dad lived in a small house, the living room, where the three of them were, opened into the kitchen which held the only house phone on this level, and Kira was yelling.

"And you thought now would be a good time to tell me? Over the phone?" He could hear the frustration in her voice. "On Monday? So soon?" She went quiet for a few seconds. "So that's why you came home." The frustration in her voice turned to disappointment. "I should have known it wasn't to see me or Mom." After another few seconds she said, "Tomorrow...yes, tomorrow," she added. "I'm sorry if that means you can't hang out with your friends." She didn't sound at all sorry. "Welcome to my world." Then she lowered her voice and said a few things he couldn't make out before hanging up the phone.

"You hungry?" Derrick asked his mom, looking for an excuse to go into the kitchen to check on Kira, to start making amends.

Mom shook her head to indicate 'no.'

Out of the corner of his eyes he saw Kira staring at the phone as if deep in thought. Then, with a swift inhalation followed by a slow, measured exhalation she stood tall, picked up the receiver and dialed another number.

"Hello, Mr. Jeffries, it's Kira," she said. "I'm so sorry—" she dropped her head forward and reached up to pinch the bridge of her nose. "Yes, sir. I know, sir. If you'd just let me explain." She stood quietly, listening. "Yes, sir. Your office, first thing on Monday morning. See you th—"

Apparently Mr. Jeffries didn't let her finish. The man was an ass. So was Derrick. By thinking only of himself and his need to get up to see his parents, he'd gotten Kira into trouble with her boss. After all she'd done for them.

When she emerged from the kitchen she walked through the living room right up the stairs, without saying a word. Derrick started after her.

"Don't." Dad grabbed his arm.

"You heard what just happened." Derrick tried to pull away.

"Have to be deaf not to." Dad looked up at him. "Fifty-four years of marriage have taught me a few things." Derrick stopped to listen so Dad released his hold. "When a woman's all fired up, especially if you're the one who got her that way, you need to give her some time alone to cool down."

Derrick looked upstairs, waiting, wondering, expecting Kira to appear at any minute, her bags and shoes in hand, demanding to be taken home. Dread filled his belly at the thought of four tension-filled hours cooped up in a car with her, especially when she had every right to be pissed at him.

Her sneakers came into view first. The rest of her followed. She'd put her hair up into a high ponytail and added an armband above her left elbow to hold her iPhone which was attached to the white earbuds in her ears. Without looking at anyone she said, "I need to go for a run," and walked right out of the house.

Once again, Derrick started to follow.

"Leave her be," Dad said.

"She doesn't know her way around, GPS won't work."

"Town's not that big," was all Dad said.

True. But still.

Derrick hurried to the door in time to see Kira take off at a fast pace, her form excellent. Based on her physique, she jogged a lot. He watched for as long as he could, before she turned right at the end of the road and disappeared from view.

Over the next few hours, Derrick busied himself by doing laundry, helping Mom with her exercises, and then occupying her so Dad could get out for a much needed haircut in town and a few hands of cards at the firehouse. By three o'clock, though, he was done waiting for Kira to return. She could have pulled a muscle or cramped up or been hit by a car. She could be lost or injured and waiting for him to come find her.

"I'm going after her." Derrick stood.

"About time." Dad looked up from reading the newspaper he'd gotten while in town.

"About time? You're the one who told me not to go after her right away."

"Wait too long and a woman'll start thinking crazy stuff and creating problems that don't exist."

Unbelievable. "It would have been nice if you'd shared that important bit of information a little bit earlier, don't you think?" Derrick grabbed his car keys and left.

A new coffee shop had opened on Main Street about two blocks down from a dollar store and six blocks before a fancy gas station/convenience mart. Growing up, Derrick couldn't wait to get out of this town. Now, he felt a tug of longing for the slower pace and peaceful quiet of small-town life. "Hey, Mr. Harvey." Derrick waved out his car window. The owner of the local hardware store had to be pushing ninety years old, yet there he stood, sweeping the sidewalk out in front of his store.

His old employer waved back, although Derrick got the impression he had no idea who he was waving to. After scanning the sidewalks and benches all through town, the playground at his old elementary school, and the track behind the high school, he took a right toward the park... and spotted Kira, lying on her back under a big old weeping willow tree, her legs crossed at the ankles, both hands up behind her head.

He pulled into a parking spot, shut down the engine, and climbed out of his car.

Kira rolled onto her elbow. Seeing him, she rolled right back into the position she'd been in when he'd first spotted her without so much as a wave or a smile or any sign of welcome.

He approached anyway, on guard, not sure what to expect.

"It's so peaceful here," she said, keeping her eyes closed. "I've just managed to calm myself down. Please don't ruin it."

Without saying a word he lied down next to her,

assuming the same position, only eyes opened so he could watch the fluffy white clouds floating along the beautiful blue sky. He inhaled a lungful of fresh country air tinged with the scent of fresh cut grass. When was the last time he'd laid in the grass, looking up at the sky? When was the last time he took a few minutes to appreciate a beautiful day?

He couldn't remember. Long hours at medical school and now work, both leading to exhaustion, kept him mostly indoors. His present life was so different from his life as a child, so cluttered with responsibilities, so lacking in time to relax and enjoy life.

"If I'd grown up in a place like this," she said quietly. "I never would have left."

"Trust me," he turned to face her. "If you'd grown up in this town you'd have been counting the days until you could get out same as I did." She kept her eyes closed, her pretty face turned up toward the sky. Derrick continued, talking and watching her. "After I graduated high school I couldn't pack up and get out of here quick enough. I'd even signed up to take summer classes at college. I'd told my parents it was so I could get ahead, before the fall semester started. But really, I couldn't stand the thought of another boring summer working two jobs, swimming in the same lake, playing in the same baseball league, going to the same drive-in movie place, eating the same boring burgers at the only diner in town." He closed his eyes, remembering. "Now...those are some of my happiest memories."

"I grew up in New York City, went to college there, work there, and live there." She inhaled deeply then exhaled. "It's not often I get to enjoy the fresh air and peace and quiet of a perfect summer day all by myself."

"You must get away on vacations."

She slid him a glance. "Nope. Mom does best when she sticks to her routine, when she's surrounded by what's familiar. And I can't afford what round the clock care would cost on top of vacation expenses."

Derrick rolled onto his side and pushed up onto

his elbow. "If you don't mind me asking, why does she need round the clock care?"

"Not care as much as supervision, assistance, and direction," Kira clarified, without answering his question.

So he asked again. "Why?"

"Severe traumatic brain injury and all that goes with it, memory loss, mood swings and unpredictable behavior. She's ambulatory, but with assistance."

"How'd it happen?"

She bent one leg at the knee and started rocking it from side to side. "I'd agreed to babysit my cousin, but I had a huge test the next day. I was all stressed out. Mom said she'd babysit in my place. She was attacked on her way home."

My God. "How long ago?"

"I'd just turned eighteen so twelve years ago."

Which meant her mother was most likely as good as she was going to get recovery wise.

Kira blew out a breath. "If it's okay with you, can we not talk about my mother? I'd like to go back to enjoying this beautiful day and pretending I don't have a care in the world."

Derrick wanted to know more. "What about your father?" Why did care for her mother fall all on Kira?

She closed her eyes and turned away. "Dad left when I was fourteen, Krissy was only ten. My mom was the most caring woman I knew. She looked out for everyone in the family, aunts, uncles and cousins included. If she could do something to help, she would." Kira smiled. "Or she'd send me." She turned back and opened her eyes. "Dad didn't like sharing her, but he put up with it until my grandmother had a stroke and Mom wanted to move her into our condo. Dad had a fit, said she belonged in a nursing home. Mom insisted, like she always did, "Family takes care of family." Dad issued an ultimatum. "It's your mother or me." Mom cried and pleaded, but in the end, Grandma had no one else, so Mom chose her." Kira swatted at a fly that'd landed on her forehead. "Dad packed up and left that night."

"That sucks."

Kira shrugged. "He set up very generous college accounts for my sister and me, and had his attorney send a check every month until Krissy turned eighteen."

"What about after your mom's injury?"

"Not a word, which was fine by me. I was eighteen, legal age to assume responsibility for my sister and my mother. We didn't need him."

Derrick said the only thing he could think to say. "I'm sorry." She'd been through so much at such a young age yet had managed to finish college and attend graduate school to earn not one but two masters' degrees, with no support and encouragement from loving parents, like he'd had. And while having to care for her mother and her sister. She was one strong, determined, and admirable woman.

"I'm sorry, too," she said. "He was a great dad up until he left. And my mom was a great mom. Even though she's still my mom she's not my mom like she used to be my mom…if that makes any sense."

It made perfect sense. Derrick reached over, took Kira's hand into his and held it.

And she let him.

For the next few minutes, they laid just like that, side by side, hand in hand, listening to random birds and someone hammering off in the distance. A light breeze blew past, the tree's long, graceful branches swayed back and forth, shading them from the sun. Derrick couldn't remember a more perfect late summer day, or feeling so comfortable just doing nothing with a woman.

Kira let out a sigh.

"You okay?" he asked.

"I will be," she answered.

"Do you want me to talk to your boss, to explain what happened?" He would, in a heartbeat, regardless of any possible consequences. Kira didn't deserve to suffer because of his actions.

"No." She went up onto her elbows. "I'll handle it."

Like she handled everything, he was sure, on her own. "But you shouldn't have to."

"Regardless."

"I'm sorry," he said, again. Never had he meant an apology as much as he'd meant that one.

"I know." She plopped down on her back, bending her knees, her sneakers planted on the grass.

They laid in companionable silence some more until Kira blurted out, "On top of everything else I've got going on, my sister has decided now is a good time to have a baby."

A decision Kira did not sound happy about. "Just like that? Is she married?" Not that marriage was a requirement or anything.

"Married? I don't even think she has a steady boyfriend. But I don't see her enough to know for sure."

Derrick did the math. "She must be around twenty-six years old which is old enough for her to do what she wants."

"You don't get it." Kira sat all the way up, crossing her legs, yanking on a blade of grass. "When she was nine, Krissy won a fish at a carnival in Central Park. I wound up feeding it and changing the water. When she was thirteen, Krissy insisted she was responsible enough to take care of a cat.

I wound up putting out fresh food and changing the litter box. Two guesses who that damn cat still lives with." Kira pointed at her chest. "Me."

"In high school," she went on, "when the novelty of a particular boyfriend wore off and Krissy got bored, she dumped him, no warning, no negotiation, done, goodbye, moving on."

Derrick felt compelled to point out, "High school was a lot of years ago. You said yourself you don't see her that often. Maybe she's changed."

"Maybe," Kira said.

"Probably," Derrick added.

Kira glared at him. "Whose side are you on?"

He smiled. "Your side, of course. I'm just—"

"Well don't." Kira wiped dead grass from her leggings. "You stick to dealing with your family and I'll worry about mine." Kira looked off in the direction of Main Street. "You know what this town is missing?"

Derrick laughed. "Do you have any idea how long it'll take me to answer that?"

Kira smiled. God she was even prettier when she smiled. "A motel."

Funny that's the only thing she'd noticed. Wait a minute. "Why do you sound like you need one?"

"I'm no longer on call and Krissy—who I have no desire to see right now—is with my mother so there's no need for me to be back to the city today. If there was a motel in town, you could spend the evening with your parents and I could spend the night blissfully alone in my very own room."

Derrick hated the idea of her spending the night all alone in a motel room. "Don't be ridiculous. You'll stay at the house."

"Your dad doesn't want me there."

Derrick sat up too. "Then why did he tell me to pick up some steaks and whatever you want him to grill you for dinner, on our way home?"

She shrugged. "That was nice of him. But I really don't have it in me to listen to how great you are and how horrible I am."

"I told him everything, Kira."

Her eyes went wide. "Everything, everything?"

He smiled. "Okay, not *everything*. But how you wouldn't talk with me until I got the HIPPA form signed and after I got it I wasn't able to reach you so I drove down to your office and so on."

"What did he say?"

"That he owes you an apology for the heartless beast comment."

"First time anyone's ever called me that." She looked down and pulled out another blade of grass. "At least to my face."

"I doubt he would have said that to your face if he'd known who you were." Although with his dad, he couldn't be quite sure.

"To be completely honest, I'm upset with my sister and stressed about what's going to happen on Monday when I meet with my boss. I'm really not in the mood to be pleasant company." She shook her head. "A nice long hot bath, a turkey sandwich, a chilled bottle of wine and I'm good."

Not if Derrick had any say in the matter. "You have another night all to yourself. You can do anything you want and you want to spend it alone in a motel room? That doesn't sound like fun at all."

She looked over at him. "For me it is."

"It's not what you wanted last night." Last night she'd wanted to spend the night with him...naked. And now Derrick couldn't shake that thought from his brain.

"Well, we can't always have what we want, now can we?"

"Tonight you can," he told her, wanting to show her a good time. This woman who took care of her mom, who'd taken care of his mom and had gotten her the service and equipment she needed, who rarely had a night to herself, deserved to have at least one night of fun this weekend. Derrick was determined to see that she did. "Come back to the house. We'll have dinner. Mom and Dad go to bed early. We can go out for drinks." Two glasses of wine and three shots of Southern Comfort with lime, to be exact. "Or we can swing by the liquor store now and get hammered out back by the fire pit behind the house later on." Under the stars, like he'd done so many times as a teenager. "*That* will be fun." He looked over at her. "And tonight, if you offer, I promise I won't turn you down."

# CHAPTER SEVEN

KIRA SAT AT the table in the kitchen, recalling how Derrick's dad had, in fact, apologized for his 'heartless beast' comment, the minute Kira walked into the house. Then he'd thanked her again for all she'd done earlier that morning, for getting a new home health care agency to come out to visit Daisy, and for not having his idiot son arrested for kidnapping. She smiled. Thank the good Lord Derrick hadn't shared his atrocious video of her.

"You're smiling," Derrick said from across the table.

"What? A person can't smile?" Kira speared a chunk of the potato salad they'd picked up on the way home from the park earlier, a scoop of which now rested on her plate.

"You been doing it a lot," Mr. Limone pointed

out around a mouthful of steak. "Sitting there all quiet, smiling."

It was the whole family togetherness thing. The four of them, Daisy propped up in her new wheelchair, sitting around the table as Derrick shared the happenings at his new family practice, his dad shared news about his friends in town, and they both argued about incidents from Derrick's youth and whose version was the true and accurate one. Mr. Limone helped Daisy, cutting her food into tiny pieces, patiently waiting while she tried to feed herself with her left hand, assisting only when she became frustrated. At times they both sat there, not eating, simply holding hands under the table, their mutual love for each other evident. Enviable. Daisy seemed so happy to be at the table, a part of their little group, smiling her half-droopy smile, actually chuckling a time or two over the antics of her husband and son.

Kira remembered dinners with her own family, Dad's hysterical impressions of his boss, Mom encouraging good manners, each one of them taking a few minutes to share the best and worst parts of their day. Entertaining Krissy would tell jokes or recount something funny that'd happened at school. They'd all laugh. Kira had felt a part of something special. Then life had changed...and then it'd changed again.

"Hey," Derrick said, reaching over to lift her chin. "I liked it better when you were smiling."

"Sorry." Kira forced out a smile. "Everything's delicious."

"So you said already," Mr. Limone pointed out.

"Dad," Derrick cautioned. "Stop it. You promised to be nice."

Even though he'd apologized and seemed to appreciate what she'd done for Daisy, he wasn't near as warm to her as he'd been prior to finding out that Kira the nurse and Miss Peniglatt were the same person. Obviously he still thought she'd only done what she'd done because his son "the doctor" had called her.

"It's okay," she told Derrick. "He's right. I did already say that." For sure she would not be saying it again. Kira focused in on eating. The sooner she was done the sooner she could leave the table and busy herself cleaning the kitchen. That'd been the deal. They'd cook while she sat with Daisy and after dinner she would clean up.

An awkward silence fell over the table.

Kira felt awful. Her presence was ruining Derrick's time with his family.

She should have insisted he take her to a motel.

"Ouch!" Mr. Limone jerked back his right hand. "Damn it, woman. You know how I hate that."

Daisy simply stared at her plate.

Derrick smiled. "Mom rarely yells," he said.

Mr. Limone added, "But she sure as heck lets you know when she's not happy with you."

"One way she does it is with a quick, hard pinch," Derrick explained.

"Which it turns out she can do just as good with her left hand as with her right." Mr. Limone rubbed his right forearm.

Daisy gave Kira a droopy yet satisfied half-smile as she slid her left hand across the table, palm up. Kira took her hand and smiled back as Daisy gave her a tight squeeze. Kira wished she could have met this sweet woman before the stroke.

Easy as that, the mood around the table changed.

Derrick said, "She's a sneaky pincher. You never saw it coming."

"Got the boys' attention, that's for sure," Mr. Limone said. "Even when they was bigger and faster, they never ran from her."

"Because she'd only get us later on," Derrick said. "At the dinner table or just as we were about to fall asleep."

Daisy said, "Nooooooo."

"Oh, yes, you did," Derrick said, with love in his eyes. "But only when we deserved it."

Daisy nodded. "Deeeserrrrrrrr…"

Turning to look at Kira, Mr. Limone asked, "So what'd your mama do to keep you in line?"

"She'd said, "Family takes care of family."" If Kira complained about having to watch Krissy instead of getting to play with her friends, her mother would say, "Family takes care of family." If she tried to get out of helping Aunt Bernice—who was overweight and on oxygen and moved slower than a sloth—at the grocery store her mother would say, "Family takes care of family." Mom said those words and lived by them until she no longer could. Then it was Kira's turn.

Daisy gave her hand another squeeze. Kira blinked back into the present, needing some distance from this happy family time. "I'm sorry," she said, pushing back her chair. "Please excuse me." She stood. "I, um." She looked down and met each of the three pairs of eyes staring up at her. "I'm not feeling so well." She put her hand over her stomach for effect.

"Hope it wasn't my steaks," Mr. Limone said.

"No. Of course not. Everything was delicious." She stopped, realizing what she'd just said, unable to keep from smiling.

"So you said already." Mr. Limone smiled too. They'd come full circle.

"I'm just going to," she pointed to the stairs, "lie down for a few minutes. Call me when you're done and I'll clean up." Without waiting for a response she turned and all but ran up the stairs.

Kira had just sat down on the bed when there

was a knock on the door. Derrick hadn't waited long before coming after her. She didn't answer, hoping he'd go away, embarrassed by her behavior. When had she become so inept at interacting with people face-to-face? At leaving the past where it belonged, in the past? At keeping her private life private?

The door opened. "You okay?" Derrick asked. Such a nice guy.

"Sorry." She turned to face the doorway. "It's been a while since I've sat down to a family dinner. It brought back…" Emotion clogged her throat. She tried to clear it. "…memories." She shook her head. "I don't belong here. I think you should take me to a motel."

He walked in and sat down beside her. "I'm not taking you to a motel."

"Fine. I'll call a taxi." She hesitated. "You do have taxis in this town, right?" She couldn't recall seeing any when she'd been on her jog earlier.

He thought for a few seconds then his full, kissable lips turned into a slow, sexy smile. "Nope."

He shook his head. "No taxis in this town. You're stuck here."

No she wasn't. Even if he was telling the whole truth, which she didn't believe he was, after all the time they'd spent together, she was ninety-eight percent certain if she insisted, he'd take her wherever she wanted to go. But even though she probably should leave and give Derrick uninterrupted time with his parents, she'd lied earlier. While a nice long hot bath would be lovely, Kira ate too many turkey sandwiches, drank too many chilled glasses of wine without being in the company of others, and spent too many anything but blissful hours alone…with Mom, which, most of the time, was pretty much the same as being all alone.

He leaned over and bumped her playfully with his muscular shoulder. "We'll have fun."

God Kira needed a night of fun.

*And tonight, if you offer, I promise I won't turn you down.*

Oh, no. She jumped off of the bed, needing some distance between her and Derrick. "Fun doing what?" She turned on him. "I have no intention of having sex with you. Last night was a one-time offer." Made to a stranger, a man she'd never see again. But one day later, Derrick knew too much about her and she knew too much about him and his family. She'd actually started to like him, damn it. Sex now would... complicate things. Emotions complicated things. And Kira's life was complicated enough.

Derrick stood, too. "We'll have fun drinking and talking, drinking and roasting marshmallows for s'mores. Then we'll play drunk horseshoes and drunk cornhole in the glow of a roaring bonfire." He walked over to where she stood, looking out the window.

"I'm sensing a theme here."

He positioned himself close behind her. "Long time ago I learned, the most boring activities turn fun when you're under the influence of alcohol."

"Good to know."

"Drunk stargazing to find the constellations."

It all sounded fun.

He stepped in even closer, pressing his front

to her back, too close, and leaned down, placing his mouth close to her ear as he whispered, "Drunk sex."

She turned her head slightly, trying to see his face. "Are you saying sex with you is boring and I'll need alcohol to make it fun?"

"What?" He jerked back. "Hell no."

Such a male response. "Doesn't matter, because it's not going to happen."

He turned on the charm, leaning in close again. "I bet I can get you to offer again."

Kira wasn't sure if it was his hot, moist breath hitting an over sensitive spot or the intent of his words, but a very pleasant tingle shot through her. Even so she countered, "I bet you can't."

"If I can't," he stepped back, starring down at her, so serious, "we both lose." Then, without giving her a chance to respond, he turned and walked toward the door. "Come on. I'll help you clean the kitchen."

A few hours later, after Kira had helped Daisy with some physical therapy exercises, reviewed a pack of cue cards as part of her speech therapy, and helped her get ready for bed, she followed Derrick down the back steps into the backyard. "I don't get it," he said, carrying a heavy cooler filled with ice and booze like it was nothing. "You're so good with my mother. You obviously enjoy hands-on patient care and you're damn good at it. Watch this last step."

While the light up by the back door was on and the flames blazing in the fire pit lit up part of the large yard, there was about twenty feet of total darkness between the two.

Derrick stopped and turned, waiting for her. "Take my arm."

How gentlemanly. Shifting the old comforter he'd given her to carry into her right hand, she held on to him with the left.

"Why would you want to spend your days in an office setting," he asked. "Making difficult decisions about patients you never see, being front and center in the ongoing battle between patients and their insurance carriers?"

The answer was easy enough. "I needed something with regular hours, Monday through Friday. It's too hard to schedule aides for Mom around a changing twelve hour shift schedule or on call responsibilities where I'd have to go out and see patients. WCHC pays me good money, which I need to cover all the stuff Mom's insurance doesn't pay for." But lately she'd begun to wonder if her large salary was worth all the aggravation. "Plus I like the business side of health care."

As they got closer to the fire, when Kira could see the grass under her feet again, she let go of Derrick's arm. "Nurse case managers get a bad rap." When he stopped, she dropped the blanket next to where he'd set the cooler. Then she picked up the cloth bag holding one of the collapsible chairs Derrick must have carried out earlier when he'd made the fire, dumped it out and opened it up. "Yes, we're fiscally responsible to our employer, but we're nurses first. Our priority is seeing that our patients get the quality care they need but in a cost effective manner."

"Your company makes money by limiting the

care your patients receive," Derrick said, setting up the other chair.

A common misperception, Kira sat down, reached into the cooler and took out a beer. "My company makes money when our patients remain healthy. About half of my case managers are assigned to health maintenance only, reminding patients to get their physical exams and take their medications, have their blood pressure and blood sugar levels checked on a regular basis."

She twisted off the top and handed the beer to Derrick.

He took it and sat down beside her. "Thank you."

"We want our patients to be well cared for and maintained safely in their homes. Decubiti cost money. Falls resulting in fractured hips or other injuries cost money. Injury or worsening health in the primary caregiver, whether or not that primary caregiver is our client, costs money, because if they're not able to care for the patient it usually means admission to an inpatient facility which is almost always more expensive than maintaining someone in their home." Facts she'd presented to Mr. Jeffries over and over again yet he remained focused only on the cost of care.

Derrick handed her a single serve bottle of chardonnay and a wineglass. "My mom and dad were left on their own for three days, Kira. Three days."

She felt terrible about that. "We're not perfect. We've got new management focused on cost containment above all else. I'm doing my best to correct the problems as they're brought to my attention while also trying to get my boss to understand..." She twisted the top off of the bottle and poured it into her glass. "You know what? I don't want to talk about it. You promised me a night of fun, and talking about my work is not fun."

"You're right." He held up his beer. "To a night of fun."

She tapped it with her wineglass. "To a night of fun." *And tonight, if you offer, I promise I won't turn you down.* Lord help her, she needed to stop thinking about that. Kira stared into the dancing flames. "This is my first bonfire."

"What do you think so far?"

"It's beautiful." Peaceful. Relaxing. She took a sip of wine.

"So tell me more about you," Derrick said.

"Like what? You already know about my work and my family. What else is there?"

He took a swig of beer. "First kiss."

Kira had to think. "Mattie Furlander, tenth grade, during gym class, beneath the bleachers."

"Missy Kerjohnson," Derrick said. "Sixth grade, down by the water tower."

"Sixth grade?" Kira laughed. "You sure got an early start."

Derrick smiled. "I'd started chasing after her in the fifth grade. She didn't let me catch her until the sixth."

He was so handsome in the firelight, so confident and comfortable with himself, probably never felt the need to put on airs or suck up to people, like Kira had to do on a pretty regular basis these days.

"Age when you lost your V-card?" he asked, leaning back in his chair, balancing on two legs.

"My what?"

"Your virginity."

"That's a little personal, don't you think?"

"Come on. Play along. I was fifteen. She was seventeen with a pretty easy reputation, if you know what I mean." He winked. "It happened in the backseat of her car and a guy I didn't know she'd been seeing at the time beat the crap out of me afterwards." He took another swig of beer then smiled. "But damn, it'd been worth it."

Kira threw her little wine bottle at him. Too bad it was plastic...and empty.

He caught it mid-air. Impressive reflexes. "Your turn."

Fine. "Unlike you, I waited until college. Freshman year." She took a sip of wine. "There were candles and soft music." It'd been perfect. But Danny had been looking for a fun-loving college girlfriend, not one responsible for her angry and rebellious fourteen-year-old sister and her brain-injured mother, which didn't leave much time left over for fun. So he'd dumped her, same as every other boyfriend she'd had. Same as her dad had dumped her mom. For being responsible. For taking care of her family. Lesson learned. Now Kira made it a point not to get emotionally attached to men, she glanced over at Derrick, which was easier said than done sometimes.

"Ice cream," he said. "Favorite flavor. Mine's coffee. Preferably with nuts."

Happy to move on, Kira answered, "I'm not all that particular as long as it's covered in hot fudge."

"Now we're getting somewhere." Derrick finished off his beer. "Drink up, slow poke." He pointed to her almost full glass. "We can't start the fun stuff until we've got at least one drink in us or it won't be fun."

Kira sucked down two big swallows.

"Atta girl. Favorite type of music."

"Anything that isn't rap."

"I like some country and rock. I used to play drums in a band."

Of course he did. "I used to play the cello." A loud POP came from the fire pit. Kira jumped.

"Relax, City Girl. Nothing out here's gonna hurt you. And the fire should keep the skunks away."

"The what?" Kira finished off her wine for fortification then looked around. "Skunks? For real?"

Derrick didn't address her concern for skunks. Instead he laughed and said, "Sports," as he reached into the cooler.

"I think we should talk more about skunks." Kira lifted her feet onto the chair like an idiot, as if a bite to the lower extremities was the worst a skunk could do.

"Don't worry." He leaned in and patted her knee. "I'll protect you." Then he sat back. "I played baseball throughout high school."

Based on all the trophies in his bedroom, he must have been pretty good at it.

"Debate team," Kira said, reaching into the cooler for another mini bottle of wine. "Science club. Interact." Her hand settled on a large glass bottle, not the right shape to be one of Derrick's beers. She pulled it out and held it up to the fire. "Southern Comfort?"

"There's some cut up limes in a baggie in there too." He motioned to the cooler with his beer.

"Boy, while I was working with your mom you were pretty busy."

"While I wasn't in the science club, like you, because in my school, guys got beat up for stuff like being in the science club, I like science."

Which explained the periodic table on the back of his bedroom door.

"And tonight," he continued. "I'd like to conduct an experiment."

"With Southern Comfort."

He nodded. "Last night it took two glasses of wine and three shots of Southern Comfort with lime, in under two hours, to get you to come on to me."

Wow. He'd been watching her more closely than she'd thought.

"Based on that," he said. "I've created a hypothesis."

"Oh, you have, have you?" This she had to hear.

"Yes I have. If Kira drinks two glasses of wine and three shots of Southern Comfort in under two hours, she'll come on to me again tonight."

She couldn't help but laugh. "Oh, you'd like that, wouldn't you?" To be honest, if circumstances were different, she'd like it too.

"Yes, I would," he said sincerely. "But only to prove my hypothesis."

Right. "Have you considered all the possible variables? Like tonight I have a nice big dinner in my belly while last night I'd only eaten some peanuts and pretzels. That may negatively affect the outcome of your experiment."

"But tonight," he countered, "I've got a nice romantic atmosphere on my side." He motioned to the fire pit with one hand and up to the starry sky with the other. He had a point. "Plus, you like me."

So sure of himself. "You think so?"

He smiled. "I know so."

"Well you're wrong." No he wasn't. "I can

barely tolerate you," she lied, liking him a little too much.

He leaned in. "How much a woman likes me is directly proportional to the amount of alcohol she consumes."

Now it was Kira's turn to smile. "Another hypothesis?"

"A fact."

"We shall see." Kira rummaged around in the cooler to find the limes and two shot glasses.

# CHAPTER EIGHT

DERRICK COULDN'T REMEMBER the last time he'd laughed so hard. For sure it had nothing to do with the two beers and two shots of Southern Comfort he'd gulped down over the last hour and a half, at least he didn't think so. "In all the hundreds of times…" he fought to catch his breath "…I've played…cornhole…" he doubled over, his forearm bracing his abdomen "…I have never…" he couldn't stop "…had a corn bag…" similar to a beanbag, only filled with dried corn kernels "…go into the fire pit." Let alone two. The second one sizzled, same as the first. Popcorn jumped out of the blaze sending another wave of laughter through him.

"I find that hard to believe." Kira stood in the shadows, facing him, about thirty-three feet away, beside the other homemade cornhole box, which was nothing more than a rectangular box, built on an angle, with a hole toward the top. "Whose idea was it to set that other box so close to the fire?"

"It's a good six feet away." He'd purposely let her pitch toward the box closer to the fire so she could see the hole better. "You can't play at night if you can't see."

Now Kira was laughing too. "Well you can't play if all your corn bags burn up, either."

God help him, his sides were starting to ache.

"I'll have you know, I have many fine qualities," she said.

"If you do say so yourself," he teased, enjoying himself immensely.

"I *do* say so myself," she said. "But athleticism isn't one of them."

"I don't know about that. You have mighty fine form when you run." He'd enjoyed every second spent watching her earlier that day.

She waved him off. "Running doesn't require any skill."

"You have to do it without twisting an ankle or getting hit by a car," he pointed out.

"I stand corrected. I am skilled at running. But a proficiency at throwing things eludes me."

"More like a proficiency for aiming at things eludes you."

"Oh, I can aim just fine," she said. "It's the actual hitting what I'm aiming at that gives me trouble. Now go on and throw your last bag, you show-off. Let's get this over with."

He held it up. "If I make this, that's three in a row. You owe me a kiss."

She planted both hands on her hips. "I think I've been hustled."

Smart girl.

He let the third corn bag fly. Swish...right into the hole.

"You and your, 'I'm rusty. I haven't played in years,'" she mimicked him. "I never would have made that bet if I'd thought you'd actually land three in a row."

Of course she wouldn't have. "A bet is a bet." To increase his odds of success, he'd fired off a bunch of practice throws while she'd been inside with Mom. Then he'd gone out of his way to pretend to suck when they'd first started playing. Did that make him a cheat? Maybe. But a man's got to do what a man's got to do to get the girl. He wanted the girl. And she wanted him.

"It was a fair bet. If I didn't get three in a row you would have gotten out of drinking that third shot." The main reason she'd likely taken the bet.

"There was nothing fair about that bet, and you know it."

He decided to ignore that comment. "I'll let you choose. Which do you want to do first? The shot or the kiss?"

"How magnanimous of you," she said sarcastically as she walked over to him, only a little unsteadily. "I'll take the shot then maybe the kiss won't be so bad."

On his way to the cooler he smiled. Nothing easy about Kira, she was a challenge. Never thought he'd enjoy spending time with a challenging woman, which is why he typically stayed away from them. But tonight he found Ms. Kira Peniglatt damn entertaining. Must be the alcohol.

"I'll pour," she said, taking the bottle from him.

"Fine. You pour." He took out two lime wedges then set up the shot glasses on top of the cooler.

Both glasses filled he squeezed a wedge of lime into each, chose one and lifted it in a toast. "To the future."

She clicked her glass to his. "May it be better than the past." Then she tossed it back like a pro and slammed the empty on top of the cooler. "Hypothesis disproved. Two glasses of wine and three shots of Southern Comfort in under two hours and I did *not* put the moves on you."

But he hadn't kissed her yet. "Too bad," he said.

"Time for horseshoes." She turned, a little too quickly and stumbled.

"Gotcha." He caught her and hauled her close, front to front. "So here we are again." Just like last night.

"I was looking forward to horseshoes." She tried to turn in his arms, straining to look toward the horseshoe pits.

"Honey, tossing around harmless little bags of corn with you is one thing. Horseshoes are heavy. In your hands they can do some damage."

"Hey." She gave his chest a push.

"Besides, you owe me a kiss." He tilted his head toward hers. "And I mean to collect," he reached down to tilt her chin up, "right," he leaned in, "now."

The second her soft lips touched his, a massive surge of yearning flooded Derrick's system. It took total concentration to keep the kiss light, to let her take the lead, when all he wanted to do was squeeze her close, slip his tongue into her mouth, and grab her sexy-as-hell ass to hold her steady while he thrust his growing erection between her sweet thighs over and over again.

Her fingers slid into his hair, angling his head, pulling him down.

*Yes. More.*

She tasted sweet and tart, same as her personality.

When she pushed her tongue between his lips, he sucked it in, played with it.

His hands ached to touch her, but he didn't trust himself.

Then she pressed her beautiful body to his,

wrapping her arms around his neck and Derrick let instinct take over, hugging her close, driving his tongue into her heavenly mouth, again and again, thrusting his hips, showing her how much he wanted her.

She pushed him away. "Stop."

He let her go immediately and stepped away. "I'm sorry."

"I can't." In the firelight she looked just as disappointed as he felt. "As much as I may want to, I can't."

"New rule for our night of fun," he said, gently setting his hand to her cheek. She leaned into his touch. "Tonight we can be whoever we choose to be or not to be." That sounded weird. "Does that make sense?"

Kira smiled. "Oddly enough, it does."

"Tonight I choose not to be related to anyone from the Limone family. Tonight I'm a Smith. Derrick Smith."

"But you *are* related to Daisy Limone a patient of WCHC and that's not the only reason—"

"No." He held a finger to her moist lips. "Tonight I'm Derrick Smith." He held out his hand. "And you are?"

"Stop it, Derrick."

"It's just the two of us. No one will know."

She looked up at him. "I'll know."

*There you have it.* He pushed out a breath. "Okay. Come on then." He pointed to the blanket. "Grab that. I'll get us each another beverage and then it's time for drunk stargazing."

She placed her hand on his forearm as he reached for the cooler. "Thank you for understanding."

He hated that, as a doctor, he understood completely. "Of course." After all, he was a nice guy. A horny, nice guy who hadn't been with a woman in months and wouldn't be getting any sex tonight, but a nice guy nonetheless.

"I saw some bottles of water in there. Please grab one for me...instead of wine."

"Sure thing." He grabbed one for himself as well.

They set up the blanket far from the fire so it'd be as dark as possible for optimal stargazing conditions. After drinking down some water,

Derrick lied down on his back first, immediately spotting the Little Dipper. "First one to spot the Little Dipper gets to choose what we do next."

From where she sat beside him she turned to look down at him. In the dark, he couldn't see her expression, but he had a pretty good idea the face she'd be making at him.

"You're all about the competition, aren't you?"

"Grew up with two brothers, everything was a competition. Lay down." He patted the blanket beside his hip.

After drinking some water she did. "You've already spotted the Little Dipper, haven't you?"

He smiled, hadn't taken her long to figure him out. Once again they were lying side by side, staring up at the sky.

"Little Dipper's right there." She pointed up, tracing it with her index finger.

"The North Star." Derrick pointed skyward same as Kira. "Big Dipper." He studied the stars, looking for, "And there's Scorpius."

"Impressive knowledge of astronomy," Kira said.

Derrick would never willingly admit how many

nights he'd laid in this exact spot as a kid, alone with a flashlight and the astronomy book Mom had bought him for his eighth birthday, studying the stars.

"What is Scorpius?" She slid closer. "I don't know what I'm looking for."

He moved his right arm to make room for her. She settled in with her head resting on his shoulder, pressed in tight to his side.

"Right there." He turned a little, lowering his face close to hers so they could both look up his forearm to see where he was pointing. "You see the curve of its tail?" He traced it with his finger. "Then up and around."

"I do." She sounded excited. He liked that.

Derrick pointed out a few more stars and constellations. Kira watched with interest, or at least she pretended to be interested. He appreciated that. He loved stargazing and hadn't had the chance to do it in years. After a while they both lay there quietly. Derrick looked over to see if Kira had fallen asleep.

She turned toward him. "I know I said it before, but it's so peaceful here so beautiful. Thank you for bringing me. It's such a nice change from the city."

"You're welcome." He hugged her close. "Thank you for not completely freaking out when you woke up this morning." He dropped a gentle kiss on the top of her head. "And for not telling the sheriff I kidnapped you." He'd damn near had a heart attack when he'd seen the sheriff at the door.

She turned on her side, cuddling in close. "I've had a really nice time tonight."

So had he. "See. It's the alcohol."

"No it's not." She leaned in to kiss his cheek. "It's you...Derrick Smith."

What?

She climbed on top of him, straddling his hips, lowering her chest to his. "I've never picked up a stranger in a bar before."

Hell yeah! He was totally up for some role play. "I saw you sitting there," he slid his arms around her, "and I knew I had to have you."

"What first attracted you?" She shimmied up a little to tongue his ear.

God help him his body went hard. "Your laugh," he told her honestly.

She lifted her head and smiled down at him. "My laugh?"

"Yes." He palmed her ass. "Your bold, loud, confident laugh." He bent his knees, shifting their position, to get her right where he wanted her. "And these." He cupped her breasts, running his thumbs over her nipples, loving the way they hardened from his touch. "The way your silky blouse gave hints of their shape each time you moved, fueling my imagination."

"They're small," she said.

"They're sensitive." He pinched her nipples gently causing her to suck in a sensual breath and tremble in response. Blood rushed to his groin. "They're perfect." He slid down, so he could take one into his mouth.

Through her T-shirt and bra wasn't enough. Derrick needed to feel her skin...taste her. "Your shirt." He reached down to its hem. "Take it off." Now. He started pulling it up.

Thank you God, she let him.

So damn impatient he couldn't take the time to pull it completely off, Derrick yanked up her shirt and bra just enough to expose her, straining to see her fair skin in the moonlight, before sucking a dusky nipple deep into his mouth.

"That feels...sooooo...gooood." Her voice had gone deep and throaty. When her arms gave out, he held her up, tonguing her nipple, enjoying her little twitches of pleasure before moving on to the other one. "Your mouth." She let out a breath. "I want it on me...everywhere."

Hell yeah. Derrick flipped them over, needing to be on top. "Whatever you want, baby." He kissed her lips, her chin, and up her jaw to her ear. "Anything you want."

He felt like an animal, fully clothed, rutting between her thighs, barely able to control himself, he wanted her so much. *Slow it down before you scare her away.* He tried to roll off.

"No." She held on tight. "Don't go."

"Shh." He bent down to kiss her sweet lips. "Just taking off my shirt." *And slowing things down before I come in my damn pants like a teenager.*

To his surprise, while he sat up to shuck off his shirt, Kira didn't lie there waiting for his return. She got busy pulling her own shirt over her head and unhooking the front clasp of her bra.

He smiled.

She must have seen it in the moonlight because she asked, "What?" as she removed her bra.

He lowered himself back down on top of her. "I like when a woman is an active participant." He took a few seconds to enjoy the feel of her naked chest touching his, her hardened nipples rubbing along his skin as he rocked his torso from side to side. "When she tells me what she wants, what she needs." He dropped his head down to kiss the sensitive patch of skin just below her ear. "I get the feeling," he whispered, "that you're going to be very active."

She bent her knees and opened them wide,

making room for him. Then she grabbed his ass with both hands, tilting her pelvis up as she pulled him down onto her. "And very demanding."

# CHAPTER NINE

THE SETTING WAS PERFECT, outdoors yet in a private, dark, and secluded spot, under the starry sky. Derrick was perfect, handsome, sexy and willing. Kira couldn't remember ever wanting a man more. And after much consideration, she'd decided she'd be a fool to let this opportunity pass her by.

*It's just the two of us. No one will know.*

She'd likely be fired on Monday, so professional ethics wasn't as much of an issue as she was making it out to be. But just in case, "You have to promise you will never tell anyone about this."

He stopped moving to stare deeply into her eyes. "I promise, from the bottom of my heart, I will never tell anyone about this."

So sincere, Kira's heart gave a little twitch.

There was something about him…something…
special. No. She couldn't let herself…feel. Sex.
That's all. Tonight only. Sex with Derrick *Smith*.
A stranger she'd picked up in a bar. A man she
could leave without looking back.

Done thinking, more than ready to get to the
good stuff, Kira set out to show Derrick just how
demanding she could be, using all of her strength
to try to roll them over, so she could take control.

"Nuh-uh," Derrick said, a large, heavy, immov-
able weight on top of her. "I'm in charge." He
kissed down the side of her neck.

"You see, that's not going to work for me." She
struggled beneath him. "I like to be on top."

"Tell me what you want," he said, sliding down
her body, setting a kiss on her clavicle before sliding lower. "What you need. I'll take care of you."

"I want to be on top." He didn't seem to hear,
apparently too busy giving her left nipple some
attention. He sucked it into his hot, wet mouth,
hard. Wow! Tingles of pleasure shot inward,
straight to her core. "After you're done with that,

I mean." No need to rush. The man was a master, an absolute master.

"Tell me what you need," he said seconds before he sucked her right nipple into his mouth. Her body actually spasmed it felt so good.

"On top," she said, having a difficult time focusing on anything but the absolute wonderfulness of his mouth. "Need to be on top." The only way she could achieve orgasm with a man.

"Why?" He slid further down her body, his tongue leaving a cool, wet trail leading to her belly button, then lower.

"I won't come otherwise." No reason to lie. She needed to come, needed release so bad she'd kill for it. Well…maybe not kill, but—

He reached the elastic waistband of her leggings. "Oh, you're going to come."

She appreciated his confidence, but—

"First from my tongue." He sat up, inserted a finger into her waistband at each hip. "Lift up."

In a move that was totally out of character, she did, without question, without argument.

"Good girl." He started to pull down her leggings. "The second time, you'll come while I'm pounding into you. Sneakers."

She toed them off. "You're a confident one, aren't you?" *Please God, if you're listening, let him be telling the truth, let him have the skill to make his words a reality.*

He yanked the stretchy black fabric and her underwear over her ankles, tossing them to the side. "After that," he pushed her bare legs apart, crawled in between them and laid down on his stomach, "you can come any way you want."

Then he was done talking, couldn't talk if he'd wanted to, his mouth on her sex, feasting, devouring, ravenous. Fabulous. To say she'd never been on the receiving end of oral sex before would be a lie. But she'd never, ever, enjoyed it as much as she was enjoying it right then, the sensation unleashing a groan from the depths of her soul. It was too much. It wasn't enough.

Kira bent her knees, lifted them, spread them even wider, giving him room. "That feels so good." So very, very good. She rocked and twisted and pinched her own nipples. His tongue shot inside of her. "Yes." She lunged up with her hips, needing to feel him deeper. "More."

He lifted his mouth.

No!

"You have no idea how much I want to bury myself inside of you right now," he said.

"Do it. Please. I'm ready." So ready. Past ready. Lord help her. Begging. She was actually begging…and couldn't quite muster the energy to care.

"Not yet." He shoved a finger deep inside of her.

"Yes."

He moved it in and out. Added another one, so good.

"More," she said, her voice not sounding like her own. "You wanted me to tell you what I need. I need more."

He gave it to her, setting his mouth on her again, even more aggressively than before, moving his head from side to side, licking, drawing her sensitized flesh into his mouth. Kira felt her orgasm starting to build. "Like that." She pumped her hips. "Just like that." She reached for his head, holding him where she needed him. "Don't stop. Don't stop."

He didn't stop, licking and sucking, plunging his fingers deep.

"I'm—" was all the warning Kira could manage before her mind shattered and her body blew apart and all she could do was let it happen, enjoy the exquisiteness, ride a wave of pleasure more forceful and intense than anything she'd ever experienced before.

If out of body experiences were a thing, than Kira had just had one, floating back to reality slowly, unhappily, not wanting to leave that place of absolute delight and contentment.

"Hey," Derrick said quietly, his voice deep and quiet, and very close to her ear.

"Hey," Kira replied, stretching, ready for a nap.

"Sorry, but if I don't get inside of you soon I think I may suffer permanent damage."

Kira smiled as much as she could manage with her facial muscles still all tingly. "Gotta warn you, I'm not feeling like much of an active participant at the moment. Feel free to go ahead and do your thing, though."

"Bet I can have you actively participating in under three minutes." He moved around beside her, probably taking off his pants.

Kira smiled big this time. "You even bet on sex?"

He climbed over her, the hair on his bare legs tickling her. "I'll bet on anything as long as I know I'll win."

"Condom?"

"Always," he said as he slowly lowered himself on top of her.

Once again, Kira bent her legs and spread them wide to make room for him. "What are the terms of the bet?"

He set the tip of his erection at her opening. "If I can't get you actively participating in under three minutes…" He dipped inside. "Anything." He pushed deeper, stretching her, filling her… so…good… "Anything you want that's within my power to give."

"Deal." Either way she came out a winner. Kira

wrapped her arms and legs around him, holding on as she rocked her pelvis, all the way up, all the way back in long, slow strokes until she took his full length.

Her vibrator got the job done. But damn, nothing compared to this. She flexed her internal muscles, gripping him tight.

He went still. "Don't do that."

"Why?" She did it again. "You don't like it?"

"Too much. I like it too much." He dropped his head to her shoulder and let out a breath. "I think we need to renegotiate the terms of our bet."

She rocked against him, clamping down on him with her internal muscles as she did.

"You are an evil woman." He pulled out and thrust back in.

"What are the new terms?"

"I can get you actively participating in three minutes only if I last for a whole three minutes." He pulled out and thrust back in again, his body rigid, like he was barely holding on to control. "I'll do better next time. Promise."

*Next time.* Only if their next time took place

tonight. Kira had accepted her fate when she'd taken on the responsibility for her mother. Rather than letting it make her sad, it made her determined. Determined to enjoy herself and to see that Derrick enjoyed himself, too, in the short amount of time they had together.

"Forget about the bet." She planted her feet on the ground and started to move beneath him. "Go as fast or as slow as you want. I had my turn, this time it's all about you."

"Oh, thank God." He thrust his hips, fast and hard. "You feel so good." His breathing came out choppy. "It's been so long." He kissed her neck. "Feel so good. Damn." He started to laugh. "I'm so far gone I'm repeating myself."

Kira laughed too, couldn't remember the last time she'd laughed as much as she had tonight. If circumstances were different, she'd want to see more of him.

"You feel good, too." He'd started rotating his hips, faster, deeper. Something wonderful flared inside of her and this time she let out a, "damn," of her own. "What was that?"

"Found it," he said, pounding that same spot over and over.

The North Star. It felt like the North Star was flaring to life inside of her.

They pulled back then slammed together again and again.

Derrick's mouth found her ear, panting. "I can't wait."

"Don't wait."

"It's too good."

Amazingly good. "Come for me," she said. "Show me how good."

Three more thrusts, so hard they moved her up the comforter, and his body went stiff as he groaned out his release, thrust again, stiffened and groaned, again, then a third time.

That third time sent Kira over the edge with him.

Derrick Limone was a man of his word.

Thank God for that.

She came back to her senses when Derrick rolled off of her, the cool night air hitting her sweaty skin, making her shiver.

"Here." He curled the comforter over them. Then he cuddled into her side, nuzzling in close to her ear. "Thank you. I needed that so much." He wrapped his arms around her and slid his knee over her hips. "I needed *you* so much."

He didn't need her. He'd needed sex, same as she'd needed sex. "Glad to be of service." *Glad to be of service? What a moronic thing to say.* Kira didn't do cuddling or pillow talk, made her uncomfortable. She didn't offer empty, sappy endearments simply because the moment seemed to call for them. They'd shared something special. But now they were done.

Only Derrick didn't seem intent on moving any time soon.

Kira tried to relax and enjoy the feel of a satisfied male body partially wrapped around her, to appreciate this intimate contact with another human being, but to what end? Tomorrow she'd be back to sleeping alone. She wasn't going to ever see Derrick again. Best to pull away now, to not get attached or start thinking about things that could never be.

She tried to roll away.

"Not yet," he said, holding her close.

"I need to use the bathroom." True, but not an emergency.

"What are your dreams for the future?" he asked.

"Dreaming is a waste of time." They never came true, so why bother?

"So cynical," he said sleepily. "Do you ever plan on getting married or having children?"

"No." She had enough to deal with. And what man would want to take on her and her mom?

"Too bad," he said, matter-of-factly. "Because you're perfect for me."

Time to go. "No." She fought her way out of his hold. "I'm not. Where are my pants?" She looked around the shadowed grass.

"I want to see you again." He sat up, calm as can be.

"No." Spotting a dark blob, she prayed was not a skunk, she reached for it. "You don't." Pants in hand, she stood and put them on.

"Yes, I do." Still on his back, he slid into his pants.

Kira found her bra and shirt. "Well we can't."

"Why?"

Because he didn't live in the city. Because she didn't have the time or energy to put into a relationship that wouldn't last anyway. Because of her mother, it always came down to Mom. "Don't do this, Derrick." Now fully dressed, she bent to pick up her sneakers. "I had a fun night. Thank you for that. But tomorrow you're going to drive me home and drop me off. Then you'll go back to your life and I'll go back mine." That's the way it had to be. Without waiting for him to respond, Kira walked to the back porch, up the stairs, and into the house.

# CHAPTER TEN

ON SUNDAY AFTERNOON, Kira entered her two bedroom condo, tired and cranky and in no mood to deal with her sister. Standing in the entryway she was hit by the stale odor of sickness and age. She missed the fresh air of the North Country, as Derrick had called it. Derrick, who'd barely spoken to her during the tension-filled four-hour ride home, other than to ask if she was hungry or needed to use the restroom and to confirm directions once they'd gotten into the city. Kira could have apologized for walking away like she had, only it was easier this way.

*Keep telling yourself that.*

"I'm home," she called out.

Her sister ambled out of the bathroom, towel drying her short dark hair. Aside from their hair color, eye color, and height, there was little resemblance between them. Krissy's figure was full, her temperament carefree and happy, and her attitude positive. "Mom's taking a nap."

Damn it. "Why is Mom sleeping in the afternoon?"

"Because she was tired," Krissy said, like it made perfect sense. She chucked her towel onto the bathroom floor.

"Now she's going to be up all night." And Kira would be up with her, not Krissy. She eyed the sink full of dirty dishes. "You couldn't wash the dishes?"

Krissy ducked back into the bathroom to put on some eyeliner and lip gloss. "I'll do them when I get back."

"Get back? Where are you going? We need to talk."

Krissy slipped in a pair of hoop earrings. "There's nothing to talk about."

"Nothing to talk about? You hit me with you're planning to have a baby and you have an appointment for artificial insemination scheduled for tomorrow morning, and we have nothing to talk about?"

"Right." Krissy emerged, finger combing her hair.

"Why now? Why so sudden? You don't have a steady job."

She jerked her head up to stare Kira down. "Yes I do."

"Working as a traveling nurse, moving from assignment to assignment across the country and to international parts unknown, is not what I consider to be a steady job."

"Well who cares what you think?"

"Where are you going to live?"

Krissy's eyes darted to the living room.

Oh, no. "You can't possibly think you're going to raise a child here, with Mom the way she is. It's not safe."

"I'll work it out."

"I know you will, Krissy." Kira hated fighting with her sister, hated that she still fell into the mother role when both of them really needed a sister. "You're smart. You're a hard worker. All

I'm asking is that you wait a little while. Save up some money. Find an apartment and a steady job that keeps you in one spot and has good benefits."

"My appointment is tomorrow and that's that." Krissy walked toward the door and started putting on a pair of black leather sandals. "I have been cooped up in this condo for two days." She grabbed her pocketbook from where she'd left it hanging on the front door knob. "You're back and I'm out of here." She opened the door, and without another word, she left.

On Monday, Kira arrived at her office a few minutes before five o'clock in the morning. So she was there waiting when Connie showed up, dressed in sweatpants, looking half asleep and not at all happy, at a quarter to six. "Only for you would I drag myself out of bed so early."

She set two very large takeout coffee cups and a white bakery bag on the corner of her desk.

"You're the best assistant ever." Too bad, after today, she'd likely be someone else's assistant. Kira hadn't wanted to involve Connie in her investigation of Sheila, but when she'd tried to log in to her system remotely from home, she'd been locked out. And when she'd arrived at work this morning, she found she'd been denied access to certain programs. A surefire sign she would be let go today.

Well she wasn't leaving without finding out what Sheila was up to.

Connie sat in her chair and booted up her computer.

Kira rolled her chair over and sat down beside her, looking at the screen. "I need you to get me into the case management program so I can bring up a list of Sheila's case management patients."

Connie entered in her password, clicked a few keys then used her mouse. "You know, technically speaking, I don't have access to that program."

Patient confidentiality limited access to files containing medical information. Kira smiled at Connie's use of 'technically speaking.' "I also know you have something going on with Richie down in IT. And you've got crazy amazing computer skills. And between the two of you, you'd figure out a way to get me in."

"Yeah, I'm thinking after I called him for help at five o'clock this morning, Richie will probably be expecting a blow job or something." She shook her head. "The things I do for you."

"Oh, no." Kira laughed. "I'm not taking the rap for that. You know I would never expect you to perform sexual favors for me." She glanced at Connie out of the corner of her eyes. "You like him."

"He's a pretty cool guy, if you can get past the way he dresses." She clicked her mouse. "Okay. You're in."

"Scoot over."

For the next two hours, Kira reviewed a sampling of Sheila's cases, old and new, and couldn't believe what she'd found. "Here's another one. Same Medicare certified home health care agency."

Connie, who'd changed in the bathroom and was now professionally dressed and ready to start her work day, looked over Kira's shoulder.

"Based on the hospital documentation," Kira explained, "physical therapy three times per week and fifteen hours of home health aide services per week were recommended."

Connie pointed to the screen. "But that says two physical therapy visits and I don't see anything about home health aide services."

"Right. It looks like the nurse from this new agency Sheila is using, without my approval, submitted a revised plan of care with one less physical therapy visit per week and no home health aide visits, and sent that to the patient's primary care physician to sign off on."

"Why would she do that?"

"I don't know. Maybe they didn't have the staff available." Which was a totally unacceptable reason to revise a plan of care. "Or maybe it's something more sinister. I need more time to figure it out." Kira brought up a document she'd hastily put together. "I searched by diagnosis and reviewed five cases, all fractured right hips, all female, all within a five-year age range. Two managed by Sheila. The other three managed by three different case managers. Sheila's patients received significantly less home care services and durable medical equipment than the other patients. And since WCHC is paid a predetermined monthly amount for each client, independent of the services used, Sheila's patients will cost us less than the patients managed by the other case managers."

"So WCHC makes more of a profit on those patients."

"In theory. There are other variables to consider, but yes. That about sums it up."

"It's not right."

It's unconscionable.

"Why aren't those patients complaining?" Connie asked.

A very good question. "They may not know they have the right to appeal." Or they may be appealing and Sheila wasn't following company protocol for handling patient complaints/appeals.

"What are you going to do about it?" Connie asked.

"I need more time to review more cases, to

compile a good sampling of data and analyze it."
Time, the one thing she didn't have. She glanced
at the clock. Almost eight o'clock. Mr. Jeffries
would be in any minute. "Would you do me a
favor?"

"You even have to ask? Later on I'll be giving
Richie a blow job for you." Her assistant winked.

"No," Kira stood. "Later on, if you do wind
up giving Richie a blow job, it'll be because you
want to, not because of me."

Connie smiled. "You're no fun."

No. She wasn't.

"Please copy all these open files to a data
stick," Kira said. "The best I can do is summa-
rize what I've found so far and forward it to the
board of directors along with my concerns. Then
I've done my due diligence. I've identified a potential problem and forwarded it on for investigation, since I won't be here to investigate it myself.
The rest will be up to them." She wouldn't forward it to Mr. Jeffries for investigation because
she couldn't shake the feeling he and Sheila were

somehow working together to bilk patients out of care they're entitled to.

Connie lunged in for a hug. "Maybe he won't fire you." She sniffled.

Oh, he was going to fire her. It was just a question of how he'd do it and when. Oddly enough, when she was able to tamp down the panic of being unemployed and losing her weekly paycheck, with all the financial responsibilities she had resting so heavily on her shoulders, she felt relieved. Her job had become almost unbearable of late. Kira couldn't work for a company that put profits ahead of patient care. Fighting about it, daily, was as exhausting as it was futile. She'd find another job. A better job. God willing, she'd find it quickly.

Kira hugged Connie back. "You know all the times I've told you you're the best assistant ever?"

Connie nodded.

"I've meant it, from the bottom of my heart. Anything you need, preferably legal, I'll help in any way I can."

Kira was summoned to Mr. Jeffries's office at three minutes after eight o'clock.

She knocked on his door two minutes later, surprised when Sheila opened it.

"Since no one from the Human Resource Department was available this early, I've asked Sheila to sit in as a witness," Mr. Jeffries said from behind his excessively large mahogany desk, his partially bald head shiny, his plump face in its usual scowl.

How convenient. "Good morning, Sheila."

The aging, well-dressed blonde tilted her head in acknowledgment. If Kira didn't have such good self-control, she'd have slapped the self-satisfied grin right off of Sheila's face.

"Please sit." Mr. Jeffries motioned to a chair in front of his desk.

Kira sat.

Rather than sitting in the chair beside Kira, Sheila stood just to the side of Mr. Jeffries's chair, looking down on her.

"I'm sure you know why you're here," Mr. Jeffries said, getting right down to it.

"Yes, sir. And if you'd give me—"

"There is no acceptable explanation for a gross dereliction of duty, Miss Peniglatt."

*Gross dereliction my ass.*

But Mr. Jeffries wasn't done. "You hold yourself up as the epitome of patient advocacy, yet you abandoned your beloved patients by failing to work on call as assigned, to be there for them when they needed you."

"Mr. Jeffries, if you'll recall," Kira said, sitting up taller, knowing it wouldn't be enough to save her job, but she had to try, "because of the situation with my mother, I have a system in place for just this type of incident. If, for any reason, the administrator on call cannot be reached, the case manager on call is to contact the other name on the call list, which is Alison, who you called, who was available, and who happily covered on call for me."

"But what if she wasn't?" Sheila asked.

Kira wanted to point out she was only there as a witness and not a participant. Instead she stared directly at Sheila and simply stated, "But she was."

"None of that matters, Miss Peniglatt," Mr. Jeffries said. "Your dereliction of duty this past weekend showed poor judgement." He opened a file on his desk. "I have here documentation of numerous incidences demonstrating your lack of commitment to our new management philosophy." He lifted up several sheets of paper then let them fall to the desk. "And your job performance has not improved, despite a counseling session for each infraction, performed by me, to help promote change and bring you on board."

Counseling session, right, if counseling session meant him yelling and not giving her a chance to speak. Although she did provide the rationale to justify every one of his 'infractions' in the space provided on the counseling sheet...if he'd bothered to read them, which he probably hadn't.

"Mr. Jeffries, I've made it clear that as a nurse, I cannot, in good conscience, be a part of a management philosophy that puts profit ahead of patient care," Kira said. Especially after hearing Mr. Limone's struggles and meeting Daisy.

"That is not what we're doing," Mr. Jeffries yelled.

Sheila put a calming hand on his shoulder.

He let out a breath. "I'll remind you, We Care Health Care is in business to make money."

Well here goes. "I'll remind *you*," Kira said. "That you work in health care now. You're no longer dealing with carbonated beverages or computers. You're dealing with human beings who are entitled to certain care as determined by Medicare." Boy it felt good to get that out.

Mr. Jeffries looked up at Sheila. "You see how she talks to me? Make a note to add insubordination to her termination documentation."

"Of course," Sheila said oh, so helpfully.

"So that's it." Kira stood. "If you're going to fire me, then do it."

"You're fired," Mr. Jeffries said.

Kira spoke to Sheila. "At least I can walk out of here with my head held high knowing I've worked hard and done my best to ensure our patients received the quality care they deserve."

"What about your responsibility to your employer, Miss Peniglatt?" Mr. Jeffries asked.

"I have had excellent reviews, every one of my years here at WCHC. Up until your arrival, Mr. Jeffries." She looked down at him.

"The cost of patient care is up eighteen percent this year."

"And my census is the highest it's ever been. Our patients are older and sicker. I have tried to show you that the majority of patients who are well cared for recover quicker and suffer less falls and re-hospitalizations, yet all you remain focused on is the cost of care. We will never see eye to eye." She turned and walked to the door, stopping long enough to say, "I'll be sure to swing by Human Resources on my way out to complete my exit interview," before leaving his office for the last time.

# CHAPTER ELEVEN

DERRICK FOUND THE address Connie had given him easily. Finding a parking spot on the tree-lined streets of the Murray Hill neighborhood had been a different story. But Kira wouldn't answer his calls? Again? Well then she should expect a visit.

Why couldn't anything with her be easy? He didn't need this hassle, didn't need this guilt, had no time…

He entered the lobby of her building, walked over to where the doorman sat behind a small desk, and held up the manila envelope filled with blank computer paper Connie had told him to bring. "Delivery for Kira Peniglatt," he said the words Connie had told him to say. "From Connie at her office."

The older man held out his hand. "I'll see that she gets them."

Derrick held the folder back. "It's a confidential file. I was given strict instructions to deliver it to her myself."

"No men allowed up there," the doorman said.

"Connie called," Derrick lied. "She's expecting me. I'll stay in the hallway." *Please don't pick up the phone and call her.*

"Go on up then," he motioned with his head. "Third floor. To the left. Look for C."

"Thank you." Rather than risk waiting for the elevator, he took the stairs.

Derrick wasn't that familiar with the city, and wasn't sure exactly what to expect when it came to Kira's apartment, but based on her high paying job and her nice clothes, he'd expected better than this. Sure, she lived in what looked like an okay part of town, in a building with a doorman, but everything looked old and dingy. And it wasn't as clean as it could have been.

He found the apartment easily and knocked on the door.

When no one answered, he knocked harder.

The door swung open. "Did you forget your—?" Kira took one look at him and tried to slam the door in his face. Well he wasn't having any of that. She'd been fired today, because of him. He was damn well going to talk to her about it. So he pushed his way inside.

"Kira," he said, stopping immediately at the look of panic on her face.

"Nooooo," a female voice screamed from behind him, fear evident in her tone. "Nooooo." Something started to thump.

"Wait outside," Kira said.

"But—"

"Please." She pushed at him, hard, then looked over her shoulder and yelled, "It's okay, Mom."

Thump. Thump. Thump.

Derrick backed into the hallway, listening through the partially opened door.

"Mom," Kira said her voice calm. "Don't do that. You'll hurt yourself."

The thumping stopped.

"Nooooo," her mom yelled.

"Shh," Kira comforted her. "He's gone. I won't let anyone hurt you."

"No men," her mother said, sounding calmer. "No."

"How about some Oreo cookies," Kira suggested. "And milk."

"I like Oreo cookies." Simple as that, her mother sounded happy again, like the last few minutes never happened.

"I know," Kira said. "Sit right here and I'll get them for you."

"Well what have we here?" A woman with short dark hair asked as she walked down the hallway in his direction. "A Peeping Tom?"

Her hair was the same color and texture as Kira's, her blue eyes similar, yet while this woman's sparkled with playfulness, Kira's were more…burdened, for lack of a better word. "You must be Krissy." He held out his hand.

She shook it, holding on a little too long. "You must be…" She studied his face. "I have absolutely no idea who you must be because Kira has never mentioned you. Or any other man for that matter, so don't feel bad." She looked him over.

"Stop it, Krissy," Kira said as she joined them. Then she focused in on him. "You need to leave."

"We need to talk," he told her.

"No we don't."

"You got fired today. Because of me."

Kira let out a breath. "Connie must have called you. She shouldn't have."

"Wait," Krissy said. "What?" She looked at Kira. "You got fired? From your job?"

"No." Kira crossed her arms over her chest. "From a cannon," she said, completely deadpan. "I got fired from a cannon."

"Oh, no!" Krissy said, glancing into the condo. "What are you going to do?"

"Don't you worry yourself one bit," Kira snapped at Krissy. "Your life will not be affected in the least. I'll take care of Mom and me and everything else without asking for or expecting a damn thing from you or anyone else!" Her eyes filled with tears. She turned away as she wiped at them. "I'm sorry. It's been a difficult day."

Derrick got the feeling her life was filled with difficult days.

"I'm not a crier." She glared at Krissy. "But I was up most of the night with Mom." She turned her gaze to him. "I left for work very early this morning. I'm exhausted, and I really can't deal with this right now. Please go." She turned away, wiping at her eyes again. "Just go."

No way in hell. He took a step toward her. "Kira." He tried to convey his understanding and concern with nothing more than the tone of his voice and a comforting hand placed on her shoulder.

He wasn't prepared for her to turn into his arms, but when she did, he hugged her tightly, holding her while she cried.

Poor Krissy, sarcastic and playful moments ago, looked lost and unsure at the sight of her big sister crying.

"More Oreos," their mother said from inside. "More."

"I'll get them," Krissy said, eyeing her sister

with concern. "Go take a walk or something. You look like you could use one. I'll watch Mom."

A chair scraped along the floor.

"Go!" Krissy hurried inside.

"Shoes," Kira said.

A pair of black flip-flops flew into the hallway. The door slammed shut.

Derrick released Kira just long enough to pick them up. Then he put his arm around her shoulders and started walking toward the elevator. "Come on. I'll buy you a cup of coffee."

She looked up at him with teary eyes and a small smile. "Again with the coffee?"

He gave her a one-armed squeeze. "Would you rather we find a bar for two glasses of wine and three shots of Southern Comfort?" he teased.

She elbowed him in the side. "You'd like that, wouldn't you?"

Damn right he would, but now didn't seem like the right time to mention it. He pressed the button for the elevator.

She slipped on her flip-flops. "Since her attack, Mom suffers from an intense fear of men, all men, regardless of age or ethnicity."

Understandable. But, "What I don't get, is why Connie would send me here if she knew—" Derrick stopped, figuring it out for himself. "She doesn't know."

Kira shook her head. "She knows my mom sustained a traumatic brain injury years ago, but she doesn't know anything about how it happened or the extent of her cognitive or behavioral changes." She looked down at her feet. "It's not something I talk about."

The elevator doors opened and he followed her inside. She stood leaning against the back wall. "Now you see why I have to keep Mom with me, why I can't take her out in public, and why I never invite men to my home. Sometimes, if a man gets too close, she'll fly into a rage and go on the attack. Other times, like today, she'll bang a body part on whatever hard surface is closest."

He nodded.

When they reached the lobby he put out his hand to keep the door from closing on her. He waited until they were out on the street before talking again. "There are new medications coming out all the time." For PTSD and anxiety.

She stopped and looked up at him. "I know you're only trying to help, but trust me, if there was a medication that worked, that I could afford, and that I could get her to take on a daily basis, she would be taking it."

"When was the last time you tried?"

"A few years ago." She started to walk. "Can we please not talk about this?"

He fell into step beside her, walking slowly. "I want to talk about it. I want to understand," why she'd stopped trying. "What if there's a medication out there that will help?" He planned to begin researching that possibility as soon as he got home. "You could get her into a day program or a facility. It would take the burden off of—"

She stopped so short, a man walking behind them almost plowed into her. "Sorry," she said as he grumbled past. Then she turned to Derrick. "My mother is not a burden. She's my mother. My family. And family takes care of family."

"But—"

"There are no buts." Kira looked up at him, standing tall and proud. "What if it had been me that night?"

"Is that what this is about? Guilt?" He stared into her eyes. "Kira, you have to know what happened to your mother is not your fault."

"I know that." She stared right back. "But what if it *had* been me? What if I was the one who'd gotten attacked and suffered a severe brain injury as a result? There is no doubt in my mind that my mother would have taken care of me until the day she died. And I will do the same for her."

He respected that, but, "Even if that means you can't have a man in your life? No husband? No children?"

Kira didn't even hesitate. "It's my choice, my responsibility. My mother is happy with me... well, as happy as she's capable of being. She's safe with me. I have three fantastic women who help me. I pay them a fortune, but they're worth every penny."

Wait. "You mean you pay privately?"

"They're very good at what they do." She took a hair band off of her wrist and started putting her hair up into a ponytail. "When you're as good as they are, you can charge what you want and insist on cash." She looked up at him. "But they put my mind at ease. My mother trusts them. I trust them. When I'm not home I don't worry. I know they'll call me if they need me. And they're a bargain compared to the female doctor and female neuropsychologist who come to the condo."

He could only imagine.

And now she was out of a job.

"You told me not to call your employer and I haven't, but I really think you should reconsider. Maybe I can—"

"Stop." She placed her hand on his arm. "If my boss didn't fire me for the on call issue, he would have found another reason to fire me. It's not your fault. And even though being unemployed makes my life infinitely more complicated at the moment, it was for the best. I firmly believe that." She turned and started walking again. "The good news is I'm a nurse. I can always find work."

"Come work for me," he blurted out the thought that'd been on his mind since he'd received Connie's call.

She stepped in front of him to avoid a dog peeing on a mailbox. "Up in Westchester County?"

She said it like he'd asked her to commute to China. "The Metro North train from Grand Central Terminal to White Plains only takes around forty minutes." Usually.

"This way." She pointed to the right and they crossed the street. "Let me get this straight. You want me to travel a good hour, each way, to work for you, because that's what it'll take, door to door, when I add in time to get to Grand Central then to my train. What exactly would I be doing?"

"Office manager. Nurse Manager. Savior of my fledgling family practice." He smiled. "I got the doctor part covered. I need help with everything else."

"I don't know anything about managing a physician's office."

They turned down a side street. "You're smart, I can tell. You'll pick it right up, I know you will."

"How many staff do you have?"

"One receptionist slash biller who doesn't have time to bill, one nurse who's threatening to quit if I don't hire another nurse to help her, and me."

"So you want me to be your nurse?"

"I want you to hire a nurse, ASAP, and manage the office. You'll be great at it. You know the business side of things, you can handle insurance companies, you're good with patients. You're perfect for the job." And the job was the perfect way to get to see her every day, to spend time with her and get to know her better, which he really wanted to do.

"You can afford to pay me one hundred and five thousand dollars a year?"

What? "You make one hundred and five thousand dollars a year?"

"I did."

"I can pay you half that, to start." If he paid himself less. "Once things at my office are working smoother and I have the staff I need, I can take on more patients. As soon as I'm able, I'll give you a raise."

She shook her head. "I can't survive on fifty thousand dollars a year."

"Work for me while you're looking for your next job. A few weeks, a few months." Anything. "Start tomorrow. You won't miss a paycheck." *And I won't feel so terrible about being partially responsible for you getting fired.* "You'll be making more than you would on unemployment. If you need a day off to go on an interview, no problem."

She was still shaking her head. "I don't like the idea of working so far from home."

"You'd only be an hour away. You trust your mom's aides, you said so yourself. Surely they could handle any situation until you got there."

She walked along looking deep in thought.

Hmmm. What would get her to agree? Then it came to him. "I'll throw in free medical care for you, your mom and your sister."

"My mom needs a female doctor."

"I'll wear a dress." At this point, he'd do anything.

She laughed. "You. You'll wear a dress." She looked him up and down as if trying to imagine it.

"And full makeup and a wig, whatever it'll take for me to pass as a woman. I need you that much." He also wanted to help her with her mom the way she'd helped him with his.

"I don't drive. How will I get from the train station to your office? Next block." She pointed. "See that red sign?"

It read Phil's Tavern. He nodded. "I'll pick you up every morning and drop you off every night." Happily.

"You need a nurse, too." She looked up at him. "Full time?"

"You'd be in charge of scheduling. But yes, I'm pretty sure I need both positions full time. Maybe even a nurse practitioner or physician's assistant to help me with patients. Maybe you could research salary ranges and which would be a better fit for my practice."

She stopped in front of a heavy wooden door. "Benefits?"

"Medical and dental."

"And free health care for me, Mom, Krissy *and* her baby, when and if she has one? Even if I only work for you for a short time then come back to the city to work?"

"Yes." So he'd have a reason to keep on seeing her, so she'd always have someone to call if she needed help.

She nodded, a hint of a smile on her face, as she pulled open the door. "That might work. Let me think about it."

# CHAPTER TWELVE

THE TRAIN RIDE up to White Plains wasn't as bad as Kira had thought it would be. Forty minutes of time to herself was an absolute luxury. But the book on her iPad didn't hold her attention. She glanced over to Krissy who sat next to her, staring out the window.

"Don't sulk. It's not forever," Kira said. "All I asked is that you give it a try." Maybe she'd like working in a doctor's office. A set schedule and reasonable hours would make it easier to coordinate child care, when and if she needed it.

"I'm not sulking, I'm thinking," Krissy said without looking at her.

They returned to sitting in silence.

Kira had managed to read three uneventful pages when Krissy said, "You know. I'm not the waste of life you think I am."

Kira set her iPad down in her lap. "I don't think you're a waste of life."

"I can't do what you do," Krissy said. "With Mom. I can't…" She shook her head, turning to look out the window again.

Kira reached for her hand and held it.

"It's too hard," Krissy said.

Indeed, it was hard.

Krissy turned back to look at Kira. "Seeing you sacrifice your life—"

"I'm not—"

"Let me finish." Krissy added her other hand and held Kira's hand in both of hers. "Seeing you give up…so much makes me so…angry. She doesn't know who we are. She's not our mother and yet you're—"

"She *is* our mother," Kira said quietly. "Even though she doesn't look the same or act the same, every now and then she'll do something or say something that reminds me of who she used to be. And if God forbid, anything horrific ever happened to you, I'd take care of you just like I'm doing my best to take care of her."

"I know you would. And I love you, for it."

"I love you, too."

"I know it makes me a terrible person, but I don't like spending time with Mom," Krissy said. "It's hard to see her like that."

"For me, too."

"But that's not the only reason I don't come around more often." Krissy looked down at her lap. "I've always felt like you don't need my help, or want it. But yesterday…when I saw you lose it in Derrick's arms, I realized how wrong I was to not even try." She looked Kira in the eyes. "I'm sorry I haven't been around more, made more of an effort."

Kira turned in her seat. "It was my decision to bring Mom home. So it's my responsibility to care for her. I want you to live life to its fullest, for both of us." She squeezed Krissy's hand. "But I'd love it if we could see more of each other throughout the year."

"I'm glad you said that." Krissy turned in her seat too. "I think I'd like to stick around a while."

She placed a hand on her belly. "To see if the pregnancy takes but also to help out."

"I'd like that."

"And for your information, I do have money. A lot of it actually." She handed Kira what looked like a receipt of some sort. "Yesterday I went to the bank and paid your mortgage for the next three months."

What? "You—"

Krissy jabbed a finger in Kira's direction. "Don't you dare tell me I didn't have to, I know I didn't have to. I *wanted* to."

"That's over eleven thousand dollars," Kira said. "Where did you get that kind of money?"

"It doesn't matter." Krissy looked ready to do battle if Kira pushed the issue, so she didn't. "All that matters is now you have one less thing to worry about." Then her expression softened. "I got your back, sis."

The gesture reminded Kira of the sweet, generous child Krissy had been prior to Mom's injury, before Kira had been forced to transition from sister to parent.

"You know a thank you would be nice."

Kira did better than that. She grabbed her sister and hugged her tight. "Thank you."

"You're welcome," Krissy said, trying to get her arms free. When she did she hugged Kira back. "Now knock it off." She pushed away. "We're almost to our stop."

When they arrived a few minutes later, Derrick was standing there waiting for them, just like he'd said he'd be. "Good morning." He smiled at them over the roof of his car. "How was the trip?"

Kira glanced at Krissy. "Good. The trip was good." It'd given them uninterrupted, Mom-free time together. A little more, and maybe there'd be hope for their relationship after all.

Derrick gave Krissy's multicolored scrub top and maroon scrub pants a quick look before his gaze settled on Kira. "You look nice." The heat in his eyes when he looked at her was totally inappropriate, and yet she liked seeing it here.

Her elegant white blouse, sleek beige pencil skirt, and matching patent pumps might be total overkill for her temporary new job, but, "My wardrobe consists of outfits like these or shorts, T-shirts, and leggings. I figured a skirt was the way to go." Besides, the professional look had given her a boost of confidence she'd really needed this morning. What did she know about running a medical practice? Nothing. But the challenge of doing something new, after so many years of working in case management, had sparked an excitement she hadn't felt in a long time. Maybe, just maybe, the opportunity to see Derrick on a regular basis had a little something to do with that.

The drive to Derrick's office took roughly ten minutes. Kira watched the route carefully. She could walk it if she had to.

"Limone Family Medicine. Walk-ins welcome," Krissy read the red, white and blue sign above Derrick's strip mall office.

"The walk-ins are killing me," he said.

"Look, there's a deli in the next plaza over," Krissy blurted out. "And a donut shop. Sweet."

"What do you think?" Derrick asked Kira, as

he pulled into the farthest spot in the lot. She liked how he left the spots out front for his patients.

"I think it's an excellent location." On a busy road. She climbed out of his car. As they walked closer she studied the other occupants of the strip mall. On the left corner was a podiatrist, then Derrick's office, an otolaryngologist, an audiologist, an orthopedist and a diagnostic imaging facility on the far end. "You're certainly in good company."

While he unlocked the door, Kira looked through the glass wall into the waiting room. Neat. Functional.

"Sara and Bonnie will be here by eight thirty. Office hours start at nine. We have a full schedule today. Lots of parents left their back-to-school physicals for the last minute. Let me put this down in my office," he held up a plastic grocery bag. "Then I'll give you a tour."

The office was set up in a rectangle with the waiting room at the top then a large reception area. There were ten exam rooms placed around the perimeter, four decorated specifically for young children. In the far left corner was Derrick's office. Beside that was Kira's office, which had been turned into a storage room of sorts. A small lab area and a medication/supply room took up the space in the center. In the top corner, facing the parking lot, a staff breakroom had a partial kitchen area with a coffeemaker, a microwave and a small refrigerator. There was also a water cooler and an oval table that could seat six.

"I can't thank you both enough," Derrick said.

"On account of you're paying us, we should probably be thanking *you*," Krissy replied.

Actually, it seemed their arrangement would work out well for all three of them, at least for the time being.

When Sara arrived, Kira partnered with her in the front to learn patient sign in and check out procedures, and the phones. When Bonnie arrived, Krissy partnered with her for a quick intro to the lab, the computer system, and everything she'd need to handle the back-to-school physicals.

By eleven o'clock, Kira was proud to note, each of them were functioning independently. Kira working the phones and reception/check-out, freed up Sara to start catching up on billing.

Just before noon, Derrick walked behind the desk to hand her a form, looking so professional in his long white lab coat with his stethoscope around his neck. "How's it going?"

Sara answered. "She's doing great. I've finally gotten through the mail from the last three weeks." She held up a stack of checks. "I'll be making a nice deposit today, boss."

"Good to hear." He smiled then turned back to Kira. "Thanks for pitching in. I know you didn't come all the way up here to answer phones."

"She's doing a lot more than answering the phones," Sara said.

"If I'm to be an effective office manager," Kira said. "I have to understand all the jobs I'm expected to supervise. No better way than to jump in and do them."

After lunch, compliments of her new boss, Kira's job responsibilities expanded when she picked up an internal call and Derrick said, "Kira, I need help in room seven."

On her way back she realized working in a patient care setting meant she could be called on to assist with a medical emergency at any time. Time to get her CPR certification updated. When she reached room seven she knocked.

Derrick called out, "Come in."

A young woman with black hair sat on the exam table, her legs hanging over the side, a little girl in pigtails dressed in head-to-toe pink, who looked to be around two years old, not that Kira had much experience with young children, had her arms wrapped around the woman's neck, her legs wrapped around her waist, and was clinging to her chest.

"I need to examine Mom," Derrick said. "But little Isabelle here is intent on playing baby koala."

Little Isabelle buried her head in the side of her mom's neck.

"Maybe you could take her to see the secret box of stickers and surprises I keep in my office for special little girls who let me examine their mommies."

Little Isabelle wasn't interested.

So Kira sweetened the pot. "I think I saw lollipops in there." While she didn't have much experience with children, she had lots of experience with distracting and bribing her mother.

Isabelle lifted her head.

Kira held out her hands. "Shall we go see?" She glanced at Mom. "Is it okay if Isabelle has a lollipop? Or maybe a candy necklace? I think I saw some of those, too." Derrick had quite a few things stashed in there.

Isabelle looked up at her mother, unsure.

"Go ahead, honey," her mom said with a tired smile.

"We'll only be a few steps down the hall." Kira held out her arms again.

This time Isabelle reached for them and let Kira pick her up. Without even thinking about it, she settled the girl on her hip like it was the most natural thing to do. Odd, because she rarely came in contact with children, let alone picked one up.

Unlike other women, she never dreamed about one day being a mom. Not with everything she had going on in her life. Yet there she stood, liking the feel of a tiny child in her arms. Something inside of her shifted.

"Kira?" Derrick's voice brought her back. "You okay?"

"Yes. Sorry." Her face heated. "We're off to the secret box." Without looking at Derrick, she exited the room.

At the end of the day, while waiting for Krissy to finish up with her last patient, Kira sat at the desk in her cluttered office, thinking about all she'd done since eight thirty that morning. She'd enjoyed interacting with the patients and helping out wherever she was needed.

Derrick was great with the patients, young and old. Professional and hardworking, friendly and caring, everyone loved him. Kira could see the potential in his practice, would have loved to help it grow and be a part of its success…if only it was located closer to her home. For now she'd have to settle for helping him find qualified staff and putting procedures into place that would help everything run smoothly.

A knock brought her attention to the doorway where Derrick stood, still in his lab coat, so handsome.

"Busy day." He walked in, moved a box, and sat down in a chair.

"Busy is good." Her mom always used to say that.

"What did you think?" He took off his stethoscope and set it on her desk. "You coming back tomorrow?"

"I enjoyed it." She smiled. "Of course I'll be coming back tomorrow." Then she got serious. "I'll give you as much notice as I can if and when I find something else."

"Thank you." He studied her.

"What?"

"Something happened when you picked up Isabelle today."

Of course he'd noticed. "I'm not used to being around children, that's all."

"You were a natural."

God she didn't want to hear that, didn't want

to start thinking about things she had no business thinking about. "Oh. While you're here." She held up a manila envelope, changing the subject. "I found these keys, but they're not labeled."

"Those are to the front and back doors. There should be a paper with the alarm code in there. I figured whenever I got an office manager he or she would need them so I left them on the desk."

Kira opened a drawer and stuck the envelope inside of it. "Don't want to leave that lying around where anyone can find it."

Krissy joined them. "All done."

Kira looked at her sister feeling such pride. "I realize today was the first time I've ever seen you on the job. You were incredible." Except for a quick lunch break, Kira hadn't seen her sister sit down once. "You acclimated so quickly. It was like you've been working here for months."

"As a traveling nurse I have to adapt quickly to new situations. But bottom line, patients are patients and nursing is nursing, doesn't matter where you do it." She looked at her watch. "We've gotta bolt or we'll miss our train."

# CHAPTER THIRTEEN

ON SUNDAY MORNING Derrick woke and glanced at the clock. Almost eleven. He hadn't allowed himself the luxury of sleeping in for months. He stretched, feeling completely relaxed for the first time in a long time.

He owed it all to Kira.

Things were stable up with Mom and Dad. The new home health care agency she'd brought in was providing quality aides and therapists and they were showing up as scheduled. According to Dad, Mom was improving a little bit each day.

In the office, it'd only taken Kira one week to straighten things out. Not even a week, four days. Patient billing was all caught up, the medication nook had been organized alphabetically, and any expired doses discarded. There were no longer boxes stacked in his hallways or dozens of messages piled on his desk, waiting for a response. She effectively and efficiently screened his calls, dealt with problems, and managed the patients, the staff, and him with ease. She'd even negotiated two contracts for pre-employment physicals and drug screening, getting him a higher rate than he'd gotten on the one he'd negotiated on his own last month.

And she sure prettied up his work environment in her classy clothes and sexy shoes.

He turned onto his side, wondering what he'd do with an entire free day now that he didn't have to deal with paying bills, managing supplies, and catching up on paperwork.

A noise in the hallway caught his attention. He listened, heard it again and jumped out of bed. Someone was definitely out there. Damn alarm system. A total waste of money. It should be blaring to scare off the intruder. It wasn't.

He scanned the room, looking for something he could use as a weapon. Heart pounding he ran to his desk. Where the hell was his letter opener?

He moved some papers around, uncovered the stapler, and picked it up.

*Great idea, idiot, a staple to the side of the head would surely incapacitate a big, burly criminal.* He heard another noise, saw the tape dispenser, picked it up and checked the weight. It'd have to do. Maybe if he could catch the intruder off guard he could slam him in the side of the head with it. He grabbed the stapler, too, backup, just in case. Then he crept to the door.

Footsteps were coming closer.

He turned the knob, carefully, as quietly as he could, and slid the door open, slowly, just a crack, enough to see a body passing by. Perfect timing! He whipped the door open, sending it slamming into the wall, raised the heavy tape dispenser high into the air and oomph...took an elbow right to the ribs. Ouch.

The intruder was small, but quick and after that lightning-fast jab he took off running. Derrick gave chase, following as he rounded the corner heading back to the waiting room. The guy's ponytail swished back and forth, long for a man.

Leggings cut off at the knees cupped a very fine, and if he wasn't mistaken, very female ass. An ass he recognized. "Kira?"

She jerked to a stop and turned to face him, doubling over, a hand cupped to her chest. "Jeez," she said, panting. "You scared me."

"*I* scared *you*?" Now that he'd stopped he noticed the pain in his ribs and rubbed the area where she'd struck him. "You hit me."

"You tried to attack me from behind…" she glanced at one of his hands "…with a tape dispenser?" Then she glanced at the other. "And a stapler?"

*Yes, well, no need to dwell on those poor choices.* He set them down on the counter to his right, behind a box of tissues. "How did you get here?"

"The train."

"I mean to the office?"

She lifted up her sneaker and wiggled her foot. "I walked. We city girls are big walkers."

"What are you doing here on a Sunday?"

Apparently done answering questions, she just

stood there, staring back at him, her gaze traveling down.

*Ah yes.* That's the moment he remembered he hadn't taken the time to slip on pants prior to confronting his burglar, and there he stood, in the hallway of his office, wearing nothing but a pair of boxer shorts.

"You live here?" she asked.

"Give me a minute to put some clothes on then I'll explain." He returned to his office/bedroom and pulled on a pair of sweatpants and a T-shirt. While there, he also grabbed the two prescriptions he'd planned to give her on Monday.

He found Kira in the staff lounge making a pot of coffee and took a minute to admire her sexy figure from the doorway. While naked would be his first choice, he sure liked it when she wore those tight fitting leggings. "You first," he said.

Taking two mugs down from the cabinet she said, "My office is a mess." She turned to face him, leaning her hip against the counter, crossing her hands in front of her. "I ordered two metal shelving units to use for storage. You approved the purchase."

"I did."

"Well, they were delivered on Friday. Since Krissy's around to watch Mom today and there weren't any patients scheduled, I figured I'd come up in clothes I can get dirty in, put the shelving units together, sort through all the papers and supply boxes, and get everything organized."

"Why didn't you ask me to put them together for you?"

She looked up at him. "Because I don't need a man to do things for me, because you're even busier during the week than I am, and I thought you were supposed to be visiting your parents this weekend."

"Change of plans." He walked into the lounge, pulled out a chair and sat down at the table. "My brother, the one finishing up his doctorate in physical therapy, flew in to meet with the physical therapist taking care of Mom."

"Oh, boy."

"Not to make trouble. Just to check on Mom's

progress and collaborate on the exercise plan." He held up both hands. "At least that's what he told me."

The coffee started coming out. Kira moved the glass pot to fill one mug then the other before sliding it back under the dripping brew. Then she prepared his coffee the way he liked it, same as she'd done for him all week. A man could get used to a woman taking such good care of him.

She joined him at the table.

He slid the prescriptions toward her.

She stared down at them.

"For your mom. Relatively new on the market. Both effective for anti-anxiety and PTSD."

"Derrick—"

He didn't let her finish. "I numbered them. First one had a seventy-two percent success rate in clinical trials, very few side effects. The second one had an eighty-four percent success rate, more side effects, but easily managed with other medications."

She set her hand on his. "I know you want to help, but you have no idea what I've been through. I finally have Mom in a manageable place. The tiniest change to our routine can ruin everything." She picked up the prescriptions and tapped them on the table. "Mom's smart. I try to slip in a medication she doesn't recognize and she'll refuse to take all of her meds. It'll be a fight, morning and night, for days, until I can get her back into a routine." She sat back. "It's exhausting."

He could only imagine.

"She'll accuse me of trying to poison her. She could get agitated and aggressive."

"You have the prescriptions," he told her. "Research the medications. See what you think. Try one. Don't try one. The choice is yours. I just thought it'd be nice if you could invite a guy over to dinner sometime, if you wanted to."

"Yeah, right. What guy in his right mind would want to have dinner at my place with me and Mom?"

He looked her straight in the eyes. "I would."

She gave him a smile so sad he felt compelled to lighten the mood. "I mean I'd invite you to my place." He used both hands to display his surroundings. "But I don't have a stove. And since you work here all week, you probably wouldn't find it all that exciting."

That got a happy smile out of her. He liked making her smile, a challenge, so rewarding when he succeeded.

"Thank you." She held up the prescriptions. "Really." She set them back down. "Now enough about me. Your turn. Why are you living in your office?"

He looked down into his mug. "I'll start off by saying everyone seems to think doctors are rich. Plenty are, but they're usually the ones who have been doing it for a while. Most of us relatively new ones are trying to dig out of massive debt from student loans." He took a sip of coffee.

"All through medical school I knew I wanted to own my own family practice. For years I've scrimped and saved what money I could to make that dream a reality. Even with a loan from my parents, when my accountant and I looked at all the numbers I realized I couldn't afford rent on this place and an apartment in addition to all of my other expenses. So I decided to stick a pull-out sofa in my office, add a shower to my private bathroom, and live here for a while, with no one the wiser."

"Until an employee snuck in here on her day off."

He was so happy to see her, to get to spend the day alone with her, he couldn't care less that she'd caught him.

"I figured it'd take at least a year before I could get my own place." He took another sip of coffee. "A house this time, something small, but with a yard where I can set up cornhole and dig out a fire pit, like at my parents' place. But the practice took off and it's doing so much better than I'd hoped it'd be doing at this time." He set down his mug. "Now I have money for a small down payment, but no time to go looking for a place."

"You could do it today," she suggested.

"No I can't. I need to stay here to help you." *I want to stay here and help you.*

She tilted her head to the side. "I thought we already established I don't need your help."

Well, she was going to get it whether she needed it or not. "You said there were two shelving units. How about we make it fun?" He rubbed both hands together. "You put together one. I'll do the other. Bet I can get mine finished before you can."

"You and your betting." She shook her head. "What are the stakes?"

Hmmm. "Winner gets to choose what we do after we're done." He gave her a look that made his choice of activity clear. Speaking of which, he'd better run and change the sheets on his bed.

"Right. Like I'll take that bet."

"You're not working for WCHC anymore," he pointed out. "Can't use that as an excuse."

"Derrick." Her voice took on a parent scolding a child tone. "You are my boss. Propositioning me is wrong on so many levels."

"The way you've taken charge of things around here, I don't feel like your boss at all. I feel like *you're my* boss, which I'm perfectly okay with, by the way." He set his arms on the table and leaned in toward her. "Lucky for us, *I* have no qualms about sleeping with *my* boss."

"Stop it."

"Fine." He sat back. "Then you choose."

She thought about it. "Okay. Got it." She pushed back her chair and stood.

"Wait." He stood too. "Aren't you going to tell me?"

She took off running down the hall, yelling over her shoulder, "I'll tell you when I win."

"Easy, no tool assembly, my ass," Kira said, frustrated, the thumb she'd just pinched in the stupid shelving unit starting to throb. "Mine is obviously defective." She glared at Derrick who sat in front of the unit he'd put together quickly and easily, smiling.

"I offered to help you."

"I don't need your help," she snapped. Then she apologized. "Sorry."

"Hey." He crawled over to her. "There's nothing wrong with needing help sometimes." He took the shelf from her hands, turned it around and snapped it into place then gave her a side-eyed glance. "Men are just better at some things than women."

She gave him a shove.

"Not a lot of things, mind you," he said, teasing. "But stuff like assembling shelving units." He moved out of reach. "Changing tires. Barbequing."

"Being obnoxious."

"Definitely being obnoxious," he said, nodding with a big grin on his face.

Easy as that her frustration disappeared. "Okay. You can help me."

"What? No please?"

Damn him. "How about I give you a—"

"Kiss?" he finished, rolling onto his back and pulling her on top of him. "Of course you can give me a kiss."

She'd missed this playful side of him and having fun with him. And man, oh, man had she missed the feel of his body pressed to hers, or, as in their present position, her body pressed to his. But kissing him was a terrible idea, no matter how much she wanted to.

He shifted beneath her, sliding her legs to the side so she straddled his hips. "I'm waiting," he said.

She dropped her forehead to his shoulder. "This is a bad idea."

He wrapped his arms around her. "On that we'll have to agree to disagree."

"We have no future together." It would never work.

"All I want is a kiss."

He wanted more, a point he'd made clear after they'd had sex in his parents' yard. She lifted her head so she could stare into his beautiful blue eyes. "What happens after the kiss?"

He cupped the back of her head, applying a gentle downward pressure. "Let's find out."

Their lips touched and Kira's resistance melted. "Damn you." She kissed him again, deeper this time. He hardened beneath her, his sweatpants and her leggings allowing her to feel the full firm length of him. Kira took full advantage of it, sitting up, resting her hands on his shoulders, rocking her hips, rubbing all the way up, then all the way down, slowly, again and again. So good.

"Atta girl." Derrick cupped her breasts. "Use me. Take what you want. I'm all yours."

Boy did she like the sound of that. "Take off your shirt."

He did.

"I didn't get to see you last time." In the dark, away from the bonfire. She ran her hands over his dark nipples, through the dusting of hair on his chest, down along his ribs. "You obviously make time to work out." She caressed his muscled abdomen.

"My second favorite type of stress release." He reached for the hem of her shirt and started to lift it up. "Want to know what my first is? Take this off."

She did.

"So pretty." He fingered her black lacy bra. "Please tell me your panties match."

"You'll have to wait and see," she teased.

In an instant he had her on her back. "I'm not

a big fan of waiting." He went up on his knees, slid his fingers into the waistband of her leggings and pulled them down to her thighs. Kira loved his urgency...and the way he went still, staring down at her body with a look of awe. "You are... stunning." He ran his fingers over her matching panties.

He made her feel stunning, and valued, and cared about. Things Kira hadn't felt in a very long time. "So are you," she said because he was, so big and strong.

He moved to the side so he could slip off her sneakers then her leggings.

While he did, Kira asked, "Remember how earlier you said I could choose the stakes of our bet?"

He nodded.

"Well, I chose loser gets her choice of position."

He smiled. "Oh, you did, did you?"

She nodded.

"I want to be on top this time." She waited to see if he'd argue. Surprise, surprise, he didn't.

But he did say, "Lucky for you I like the bottom, too," as he laid down on his back. "Now get over here." He reached for her.

"Nuh-uh-uh." She scooted out of reach. "I'm in charge."

He went up on his elbows. "No one said anything about you being in charge."

"Well, I'm saying it now." God how she wanted to be in charge of him, to bring him to the brink of orgasm again and again before letting him come. "Lay down, big guy." She pushed on his shoulder. "I think you'll like me being in charge."

"We'll see. And I get to be in charge next time."

She tugged on the waistband of his sweats. He lifted his butt so she could pull them down.

She kissed his erection through the fabric of his boxers, looking up at him as she did. "Next time?"

Still up on his elbows, he watched her every move. "Yeah, next time."

So confident. She reached in through the opening, pulled him out, and took him between her lips. She swirled her tongue around his sensitive tip again and again before taking him deep once, twice, three times, her hand working in tandem with her mouth.

He closed his eyes, dropped his head back and drew in a long, deep breath.

She lifted off of him. "You think you'll have energy left over for a next time?" She cupped his balls, rolled them then squeezed them oh, so gently.

He opened his legs wider then flashed her a sexy grin. "Baby, we've got all afternoon."

Hours later Kira lay wrapped in Derrick's arms, in his bed, exhausted, but the best kind of exhausted, content, and...happy.

"That makes three next times," he said groggily and proudly at the same time.

After giving her control the first time, he'd taken control each of the three times after that, and Kira hadn't minded one bit. "You're the man," she teased.

"Damn right I am." He hugged her close, his front pressed to her back.

In between rounds two and three they'd cleaned up her office. Between rounds three and four they'd ordered in Chinese food. But now it was getting late. "I've got to go."

He held her tight. "No."

"Really." She tapped his arm.

He didn't budge. "Stay the night. Krissy can bring you clothes tomorrow."

Kira had already spent too much time away from home over the past week. If Mom's increased agitation was any indication, she'd noticed. "I can't."

He released her.

Forty minutes later he walked her to the train platform. "I hate the idea of you having to travel back to the city alone at night."

"I'll be fine." Appreciating his concern she gave him a big hug.

He nuzzled in close to her ear. "I wish you could have stayed the night with me."

"In your office?" she teased.

"In my bed."

She'd already spent too much time in his bed… too much time thinking about all the things she liked about him…wondering… It had to stop. Or she would get her heart broken for sure.

Men didn't stick around, not in Kira's world.

"Next weekend," he said. "We'll plan ahead. Ask Krissy to watch your mom."

The train whistle sounded, signaling its approach.

"I can't."

The front of the train rumbled past.

"Can't or won't?" he yelled over the noise.

The doors opened. Passengers exited. As soon as she could, Kira boarded, without answering Derrick's question.

# CHAPTER FOURTEEN

ON MONDAY MORNING Kira arrived at work and greeted Derrick like nothing had happened between them, like she hadn't spent hours in his arms, naked and breathless, the day before. On Tuesday and Wednesday she did her job and looked after him like nothing had changed. But something *had* changed. Derrick wanted more, the intensity of his desire was so strong it was starting to become a dangerous distraction. Seeing her every day and not being able to touch her was pure...torture.

By Thursday, after two patients, one pharmaceutical sales rep, and his old neighbor Jeff, who'd stopped by to borrow his car, all inquired about the availability of his sexy new office manager, Derrick had had enough.

She wasn't available, damn it. If she was, she'd

be his—despite all the challenges they'd have to overcome to be together. He'd make it work. He'd compromise. He'd do...anything. A primal urge to claim her raged inside of him. He paced his office, antsy, needing an outlet, a release.

Someone knocked on his door.

He called out, "Come in."

Kira stuck her head in. "Last patient is out, phones are on answering service, and the front door is locked. We are officially closed for lunch."

"I need you."

She looked over her shoulder. "I was going to run to the deli with Krissy. Can it wait?"

In two big strides he reached her, pulled her into his office, and shut the door. "No." He pushed her up against the wall, his body flush with hers, and kissed her, hard. Needy.

She wouldn't give him more than sex? Fine. He'd take sex. Now.

Hands clamped to her ass he lifted her and carried her to his desk.

"What are you doing?"

He pushed aside papers, his inbox and outbox,

and whatever else was in the way to make a clear space for her.

"Derrick."

He set her down, looked deep into her eyes. "I need you," he said again. "Now."

"No."

"Yes." He clutched the sides of her head, kissing her again, deeper this time. He slid his leg between her thighs, tried to spread them wide, to let her feel his erection, to show her how much he burned for her, to make her burn for him.

For the first time since he'd seen her in one, he hated the tight, figure hugging skirts she wore.

"Derrick, stop," she said, so calm while he felt on the verge of losing it.

He didn't want to stop, damn it! But he forced himself to step back, couldn't look at her, didn't want to watch her leave.

She picked up his phone. "Hey, Krissy. Derrick and I need to go over a few things. Would you bring us back two of the specials?"

What? He turned.

She winked at him. "Just put them in the

kitchen." Phone balanced between her shoulder and her ear, she used both hands to start unbuttoning her blouse. "We'll be out in a little bit."

Derrick ripped off his lab coat like it had caught fire and tossed it onto the couch.

"The door," she whispered, pointing, as she hung her shirt on the back of his chair. "Honestly," she said, undoing the back of her skirt. "As if I'd let you get me all wrinkly." She slipped it off, draped it neatly over the arm of the chair, then stood tall wearing nothing but a satiny light purple bra and pantie set, a pair of killer black heels, and a smile. "I'm guessing you'd like me to keep the heels on."

Derrick felt about to explode. "You're damn right I would." He picked her up. "Wrap your legs around me." She did. He palmed her ass, pulled her close, and thrust his rock hard erection against her. "You feel what you do to me? How much I need you?"

She ran her fingers through his hair, angling his head. Leaning in she whispered, "That's quite a hard-on you've got going there. What do you plan to do with it?"

He laid her down on the desk, ran his hand over her breasts, across her flat abdomen, beneath the waistband of her pretty panties, down between her silky, wet lips. "I'm going to put it right here." He slid a finger inside of her, finding her hot, wet and ready. His balls tingled with anticipation.

"Do it." She spread her legs wide. "Now."

Derrick unbuttoned his pants with shaky hands, letting them fall to the ground so he could kick them off. That's when he remembered. "Do. Not. Move." He ran to the bathroom, sliding off his underwear with one hand and grabbing a condom from the drawer in the vanity with the other. On his way back he ripped the damn thing open with his teeth and started rolling it on.

He returned to find her naked, her body absolute perfection.

The condom securely on, he pushed between her legs then inside of her, fast and deep, knowing she was ready, unable to take it slow. "God help me you feel good." In and out, in and out, over and over.

She reached down between her legs and fondled herself. He watched, seeing what she liked before pushing her hands away and taking over.

"Yes," she said, clamping her legs around him. "Like that."

He moved his fingers and hips, his body a machine, programmed to give pleasure and receive pleasure. Right now those were the only two things that mattered.

His orgasm started to build. He could feel it, wanted it, *needed* it.

"Come on, baby." He moved his hips and fingers faster. "Come for me."

Her breathing heavy, Kira rocked up and down, bit her lip and moved her head from side to side.

In and out, in and out, again and again.

When she arched her back, stiffened and let out the most gratifying of groans, Derrick let go, pouring himself into her, wishing she could feel it, that there was no barrier between them.

His heart pounding, his body spent, he laid his

upper body on top of her, his elbows taking most of his weight, still buried deep inside of her. He kissed her cheek. "Thank you."

"Did something happen?" she asked, running her fingernails up and down his back.

He didn't want to talk about it.

"Hey." She bucked her hips. "Look at me."

He lifted his head.

She studied his face. "Something upset you."

"I don't like other men asking about you." He leaned down to tongue her ear. "I want to tell them you're mine." He moved down to kiss her neck. "I want you to actually *be* mine."

With a hand on each side of his head she lifted him. "If you want me, I can be yours between the hours of nine to five, Monday through Friday. That's the best I can do."

It wasn't enough, but he'd take it, for now. "I want you."

Usually Derrick didn't settle, he identified what he wanted—in this case Kira—then went after it with unbridled determination. But that approach wouldn't work with Kira. So he'd be patient, bide his time until he could figure out a way to get more. He had no doubt the wait would be worth it.

For the next two and a half weeks he and Kira 'ate lunch' in his office, most every day. The staff probably had a good idea of what they were really doing, but they had too much respect for Kira, and maybe for him too, to say anything about it. At night and on the weekends, he and Kira talked for hours, about so many different things, some funny, some sad, everything but the future. Every time he brought it up she stopped talking.

And he began to wonder if agreeing to her terms was a good idea. He wasn't any closer to figuring out a way for them to be together than he'd been two and a half weeks ago. Every request to see more of her, denied. Every suggestion for change, shot down. And while, with each passing day, Derrick fell more in love, Kira showed him nothing more than a hot sexual attraction, which, with another woman, would have been great. But he wanted Kira long term. A man of his age and experience knew when he'd found the woman he wanted to spend the rest of his life with. Only he could feel himself running out of time, and he didn't like that feeling one bit.

Late on Thursday afternoon, when he couldn't find Kira anywhere, he searched out Krissy. "Did Kira run out for something?"

"Shoot." Krissy shifted the blood-draw carry-all into one hand and her laptop into the other. "You were in with a patient. Then I got crazy busy. She told me to tell you she had to run home. The aide called. Mom spiked a temperature or something and was acting all crazy."

Jeez. "How did she get to the train?"

"Sara took her."

Good. "Do you need to go, too? We can manage—"

Krissy shook her head. "Don't look so worried. Kira will handle it."

For as much as he liked Krissy and appreciated all of her hard work on the job, he hated that her laissez-faire attitude let responsibility for their mother fall solely on Kira's shoulders, part of the reason he and Kira couldn't be together like a normal couple. "I get that Kira will handle it, but she shouldn't have to do it all alone."

Krissy looked up at him. "I've got dinner plans. Kira said—"

"Let me guess. She said, "Don't worry. I'll handle it." Like she always does. And you let her, because that's what *you* always do."

"Wait just a minute—"

No. He would not wait just a minute. Enough was enough. "If you think going out to dinner with your friends is more important than helping your sister take care of your mother, fine. That's your decision. But you won't be going out to dinner until after you help me with something, and you can't help me until after we finish with our patients, so back to work." He turned and left without giving her a chance to respond. But for the rest of the day he couldn't shake the feeling something bad was about to happen.

Around six thirty, Kira looked down at her cell phone, expecting to see Derrick's number come up—after talking with him briefly earlier, he'd promised to call back after work. But she was equally happy to see Connie's smiling face on her screen, something her old assistant had programmed to happen every time she called.

Of course Kira accepted the call. "Hey, Connie."

"Hey, hon. How's it going?"

"Not so good." She looked over to where Mom sat in her recliner chair, watching television. "Mom's sick."

"That sucks. Then you won't be able to meet up with me to celebrate?"

"Celebrate what?"

"Mr. Jeffries got fired today," Connie said. "I heard they threatened him with legal action if he didn't leave quietly."

What? Kira had received a call from her old boss, Mr. Regis, the CEO prior to Mr. Jeffries, who'd agreed to come out of retirement, along with Kira's predecessor, April Weir, to perform a covert audit based on the documentation she'd sent to the board of directors. He'd asked her dozens of questions, which she'd answered honestly, and then...nothing.

"What happened?"

"Word is..."

Kira smiled. Of course Connie had the inside scoop.

"...was in the process of forming alliances or something with the heads of home health care agencies around the state. Apparently he offered to make them preferred providers so they'd get first dibs on WCHC referrals along with kick-backs in return for limiting home health care services and medical equipment referrals wherever they could."

The bastard. "What about Sheila?"

"At first she claimed she didn't know anything about it, the skeezeball. Then Richie told me that Michael told him that while he was doing some random computer stuff next door to the conference room he overheard Mr. Regis confront Sheila about a bunch of statements from patients who said they'd filed complaints and appeals with her and then heard nothing back. Mr.

Regis pointed out he couldn't find any of those complaints or appeals. Well, knowing she was caught, Sheila turned on Mr. Jeffries like the rat that she is, claiming he used sex to manipulate her and she felt her job would be in jeopardy if she didn't go along. You have no idea how much I hate her. Anyway, now she's sucking up to anyone in power who will listen, vowing to clean up the case management department, blah, blah, blah, make me sick."

Needing to move, Kira walked out of the living room and started to pace up and down the hallway. "Do you think they'd honestly promote her?" For some reason, Mr. Jeffries hadn't given Sheila the Director of Case Management position.

"No way in hell. Mr. Regis agreed to serve as interim CEO until a replacement can be found. Richie says they probably want to handle things internally, keep it from going public."

Kira's phone buzzed. She moved it from her ear to look at the screen, her heart skipping a beat. "Connie, I've got to go. Mr. Regis is calling me."

An hour later, Kira sat in the chair beside her mom's recliner, reeling over what her old boss had told her. And what he'd offered her.

The house phone rang. Kira got up and hurried into the kitchen to answer it, expecting Derrick. But why would he be calling on her house phone? "Hello?"

"Miss Peniglatt? This is Harold downstairs at the desk. A Dr. Limone is here to see you."

Derrick? Here? She glanced at Mom, finally calm. Krissy had gone to dinner with friends straight from work. Kira couldn't leave. "Please tell him—"

"Don't you mean her?" Harold asked.

"Her?"

"Yes, Miss. This here Dr. Limone is a she."

Kira smiled as she remembered.

*"I'll throw in free medical care for you, your mom and your sister."*

*"My mom needs a female doctor."*

*"I'll wear a dress."*

Her eyes filled with tears. He'd come. Just like he'd said he would. Without her even asking.

"Please." She sniffled. "Send her up." She loved him so much her heart actually hurt. Although she couldn't be quite certain whether the hurt was caused by so much love or the pain of knowing nothing would ever come of it. The closer they got, the more she knew she needed to put a stop to their lunchtime trysts and intimate phone calls. It wasn't fair to him...or to her.

She opened the door and stood in the hallway, waiting, completely unprepared for the sight of him walking toward her, his gait in no way feminine, carrying his briefcase. He wore a flowy, multicolored dress that fell to a few inches above his ankles, which were covered in thick navy blue tights that disappeared into his sneakers.

"I know," he said, looking down. "The sneakers don't match." He said it like he'd really wanted to match, and she fell a little bit more in love with him. "But I have size thirteen feet. That's a men's thirteen. We tried dozens of pairs of women's shoes and couldn't find any suitable ones that fit, except for a pair of bright red heels, if you can believe that. But no way am I wearing heels."

She ran to hug him. "We?"

"I made Krissy come to Goodwill to help me put an outfit together." He hugged her back. "It was the least she could do."

"She *did* ask if I wanted her to come right home." Kira wasn't ready to release him yet, so she didn't. "But I knew she had plans to meet up with some friends she hasn't seen in a while. Why should we both have to sit around the condo?"

"You're too nice." He gave her a squeeze. "How's your mom?"

"Resting." She stepped back to get a good look at his face. Foundation covered any hint of razor stubble. Black liner and purple shadow highlighted his eyes, blush brightened his cheekbones, and a red lipstick colored his lips. "I like you better as a man, but you make an okay looking woman." Not drag queen pretty, but passable. Her gaze dropped to his breasts.

"I know." He nodded proudly as he caressed his womanly form. "They look real, right?"

She couldn't help but laugh.

"What?" he asked, obviously offended.

"So big?"

"Krissy and I decided I was a big guy so I needed a big rack." He adjusted his rack. "You should see the size of the bra I've got on. I could launch watermelons with it." He twisted. "It looks cool, but it's not all that comfortable. I don't know how you women do it."

She poked one of his boobs. "What have you got in there?"

"Socks," he said, itching his head through a black page boy wig then fussing with his synthetic bangs. "The lady at Goodwill is going to have one very unhappy customer at her register first thing tomorrow morning if I find anything crawling on my scalp when I take this wig off later."

Kira covered her mouth to keep from howling in laughter.

"Yeah, very funny. I did all this for you." He motioned up and down in front of himself. "You should see the contraption we had to rig up to keep the tights from falling down around my ankles. The crotch is hanging down by my knees."

Kira couldn't hold it in any longer. She laughed out loud. It felt especially good after all the stress and worry of the past few hours. She wanted to tell him how much she appreciated him and loved him. But admitting that would be a huge mistake. So she settled for a sincere, "Thank you." It wasn't enough. *It'll have to do.*

"You're welcome." He looked down at her. "You going to let me in?"

That's when Kira realized she was blocking the door. "I don't know." She glanced over her shoulder. "I just got her quieted down."

"Let me in," he said, his voice calm, his big warm hand cupping her cheek. "Let me examine her."

"But what if…" she recognized that he was a man. "She might…" hurt him or hurt herself.

"It's going to be fine," he said, so sure of himself. "At least let me try."

She wanted him to try, really, but…

He placed his hand on her arm and applied a gentle pressure. "You're going to need to move."

"Wait. Let me get something." Kira ran to

her room, unlocked the cabinet where she kept Mom's meds, and grabbed an injectable sedative and a syringe, just in case. Then she returned to the door. "Okay." She held up her hand.

"You're not going to need that."

"Let's hope you're right." Better to be prepared than unprepared.

Derrick followed her into the living room. Lord help her, he was taller than any woman Kira had ever met. *Please don't let Mom notice.*

When they reached Mom's recliner, Kira said, "Mom, the doctor's here to see you."

Mom turned her head slowly, blinking, as if trying to focus.

*Please don't focus too hard.*

"Mrs. Peniglatt," Derrick said. His voice came out deep.

Mom's eyes went wide and wary as she shifted in her chair, moving away from him.

Kira clutched the syringe.

Derrick cleared his throat. The next attempt came out higher, like a woman with a head cold accompanied by a sore throat. "I'm De...Debbie Limone. Dr. Debbie Limone. Kira said you weren't feeling well."

Mom glanced at Kira nervously.

"It's okay," Kira told her. "I'll be right here the whole time."

With that reassurance, Mom relaxed a little bit. And Derrick got to work. He took his time and explained what he was about to do before he did it. So kind and gentle. Mom watched his every move, staring at his face, his eyes in particular, concentrating longer and harder than she had in years. Derrick spoke softly in his strange new voice, the sound almost mesmerizing Mom. She didn't fight or argue. Just kept staring.

Before Kira knew it, Derrick was packing up. "It was very nice meeting you, Mrs. Peniglatt," he said.

Mom turned her attention back to the television.

"We can talk in the kitchen." Kira walked that way. Derrick walked beside her, a big, cocky smile on his face. "What?" she asked.

"Your mom totally bought it." He'd lowered his voice back to normal.

"Shh." Kira pushed him into the kitchen then peeked around the corner. Thank goodness Mom hadn't heard. When she turned around Derrick was there, pulling her into a hug.

"And how are you?" he asked as he dropped a kiss on the top of her head.

She cuddled into his embrace, loving the feel of his strong arms wrapped around her, trying to ignore the feel of his 'big rack' pressing up against her chest. "I'm fine." Now. "Thank you for coming."

"I promised I would," he said, lifting her chin, looking into her eyes. "I'll always be here for you if you need me. No matter what."

The honesty in his eyes and the sincerity in his tone gave Kira a sense of security she hadn't felt in over a decade.

# CHAPTER FIFTEEN

ON MONDAY MORNING, Derrick busied himself at his desk, waiting for Kira, looking forward to her arrival as much as he was dreading it.

On exam, her mother's lungs had been clear, her abdomen soft with good bowel sounds, and her ears, nose, and throat within normal limits. She was urinating and moving her bowels regularly without complaint. His initial thought was she'd picked up a virus of some sort that would run its course and in a few days she'd be back to her usual self.

That'd gotten Kira nervous about what types of germs she and Krissy were bringing home as a result of working in a doctor's office. At which time Derrick took the opportunity to remind her she had three different aides caring for her mother. Any one of them could have unknowingly exposed her mother to a virus.

On Friday, her mom still running a temperature, Kira had taken the day off.

Fine. No problem.

On Saturday, Krissy had pulled him aside to see if he and Kira were fighting. Apparently she'd been especially quiet and withdrawn on Friday night.

Not a good sign.

While writing a note to remind himself to call Mr. Simmons about his liver function tests, Derrick felt someone watching him. He looked up to see Kira standing in his doorway.

"Morning." She gave him a small smile that didn't reach her tired eyes. She held a business-sized white envelope in her hands. A resignation letter, he had no doubt. "Do you have a few minutes?"

*Don't do this.*

He wanted to say, "No, now get to work," then avoid her all day, all week if necessary, just so he wouldn't have to hear what she was about to say. But eventually she'd track him down. So he said, "Sure," motioning to the chairs in front of his desk. The desk where he'd made frenzied love to her not too long ago. "Sit."

"I'd rather stand." She reached out to hand him the envelope.

He didn't take it.

She set it down in front of him. "I'm giving notice."

"God, Kira." He stood. "Don't do this."

"I can't be so far away from my mother."

"The aide called. You rushed home. Everything worked out fine."

"But what if it was something more serious?" She looked up at him. "I paced that platform for twenty minutes waiting for the train, worrying myself sick. What if she flew into a rage and hurt herself or heaven forbid the aide? What if she needed emergency care and the aide had to call an ambulance and it took me an hour to get to her? What then?"

"You can't be with her twenty-four hours a

day," he pointed out. "Even if you were working in the city it would take you time to get to her."

"Yes, but I'd be a taxi or subway ride away. I wouldn't have to beg for a ride then wait for the train and sit there all stressed out while it made stop after stop, each one delaying my arrival to the city where I'd then have to grab a cab or catch the subway to get home. Have you ever tried to catch a cab outside of Grand Central Station? Good luck."

"So that's it, then. Your mind is made up."

She wouldn't look at him. "I'll stay until I've hired and trained my replacement."

He didn't want a replacement. He wanted her. "What will you do for a job?"

She walked over to his bookcase and pushed in a medical journal that didn't line up with the rest. "WCHC offered me my job back." She glanced over. "With a raise."

He plopped down into his chair, realizing he would never be able to pay her what she's worth... and he wasn't enough to make her stay.

"It's too good an offer to pass up," she said, staring at the row of journals.

"Of course it is." He didn't care, but asked anyway, "What happened?"

"Your mother's inadequate home health care plan alerted me to a bigger problem within the company. I was only able to do a preliminary investigation before my boss fired me, but I'd forwarded what I had to the board of directors. They investigated further. The results of that investigation led them to terminate the CEO and offer me my job back."

"With a raise." Lucky Kira. He should be happy for her, but he couldn't get past the misery of losing her. Because no doubt in his mind, today, when she left his office, it'd be for the last time. And not only would she leave her office manager's job behind. She'd also be leaving him.

"With a raise," she repeated quietly.

"What about us?"

"I told you we had no future, Derrick," she answered. "This is for the best."

"No it's not."

She still wouldn't look at him. "Better to end things now, before it gets any harder."

"It can't possibly get any harder." He stood again. "I'm in love with you." He walked toward her. "I love you, Kira." He took her hands in his, bringing them up to his mouth for a kiss. "We can figure out a way to make this work." *Fight for us, damn it.*

"We can't." She shook her head. "I have a responsibility to take care of my mother. She will always come first in my life."

"What life?" he raged. "You have no life. You go from work to home and home to work. You can't be happy."

"I'm not *un*happy," she said calmly.

"And that's good enough for you? To live a life that's not unhappy as opposed to one that's happy? One that includes a man who loves you? A man who understands your responsibility to your mother, who accepts it and wants to help? We can find a way—"

"No."

Damn it. Derrick wanted to shake her. "You won't even try?"

"Don't you get it?" She threw up her hands. "I *have* tried. Not recently, but early on."

"None of those men were me," he told her.

"I know you think you're different." Her eyes softened. "In many ways, you are. But over time you'll want to see more of me. You'll start to resent all the time I spend with my mother, time you can't be a part of. We'll fight. And just when I allow myself to believe it will work, just when I allow myself to fall in love and dream of a future with you, you'll leave."

"No I won't."

"You will!" Tears filled her eyes. "Like every man in my life before you has, and I can't go through that again." She shook her head. "I won't. It's too…hard. We end now. Today."

"If you need to go back to work in the city, fine. I understand. But why do we have to end? I can visit as Debbie. We can get your mom used to me. Then gradually I'll transition into Derrick.

Step by step. Lose the boobs one week the skirt the next. The wig."

She shook her head, blotting her eyes with a tissue she'd taken from his desk. "For a normal person, sure, great idea, but my mother's memory is impaired. She won't remember. Each time you come to visit will be like the first time she's met you. It won't work."

How could she be sure if she wouldn't even try? Damn frustrating woman. And that made him mad. He strode to his desk, picked up her resignation letter and ripped it down the middle. "Fine. If you're worried about being so far from your mom, if you're so certain I'm like every other man before me that you won't even give me a chance to prove you wrong, then leave today. There's no need for you to stay." He couldn't bear the thought of seeing her every day and not being able to taste her or touch her, of knowing she didn't care for him as much as he cared for her, knowing her presence had an end date and there was nothing he could do to make her stay.

"But—"

"You have a great job waiting for you. Go," he said, louder than he'd intended. "I managed to get by without you when I started my practice, I can do it again now." Of course it'd be easier now after all the hard work she'd done to get things organized and running smoothly.

"I'm sorry," she said again.

And he lost it. "Not sorry enough to try anything that might give us a chance." He loved her and hated her at the same time.

"You don't understand." She sounded weary. "I *have* tried. And I don't have it in me to try again. My heart..." she clutched her hand to her chest, "my heart can't handle another failed attempt."

He didn't want to hear anymore. "Get out." He pointed to the door.

She just stood there.

"Fine. You're fired. Your services are no longer needed. I'll send your final check home with your sister. Goodbye. Have a nice life." Since she wouldn't leave his office, he did.

As mad as he was, he didn't want Kira walking to the train station in rush hour traffic. So he asked Sara to drive her and Bonnie to cover the desk while she did.

Kira returned to her job at WCHC on Wednesday. Although she'd been thrilled to see Connie and most of the members of her staff again, by the following Wednesday she missed working at the family practice something fierce. She missed riding the train with Krissy, missed Sara and Bonnie, missed the patients. But most of all, she missed Derrick.

"For the record, I think you're an idiot," Krissy said, from across their kitchen table. "Derrick is a great guy. He's crazy about you and you dumped him like yesterday's trash."

Kira could have argued, but she didn't have the energy. "How is he?"

"Grumpy." Kira pushed away her plate and sat back in her chair. "Same as you."

"It was for the best." Maybe if she said it enough times she'd believe it.

Krissy shot her a knowing look. "Thinking that help you sleep better at night?"

Despite feeling a bone deep exhaustion, all the time, Kira couldn't sleep. Somehow Krissy knew.

"Damn it, Kira." Krissy crumpled up her napkin and threw it onto the table. "You're the smartest, strongest, most resourceful person I know. If anyone could find a way for you and Derrick to be together, you can. Yet you won't." Krissy studied her with narrowed eyes, as if trying to see deep into her mind. "Why?"

Because she loved Derrick, because the longer their relationship lasted the more that love would grow...the more it would hurt when he left, like all the men in her life always did. But she wouldn't share that fear with Krissy. Instead she said, "For starters, how about he lives and works up in Westchester County and Mom and I live here?"

"So you move." Krissy made it sound like it was no big deal. "What's keeping you here?"

"Martha, Ingrid, and Tippy." The three aides who covered the shifts working with Mom.

"You're nice to them and you talk to them but you're always so busy planning, managing and scheduling you don't really listen, do you?" Krissy crossed her arms over her chest.

Feeling parched, Kira reached for her glass and took a sip of iced tea. "What are you talking about?"

"Tippy. She's been here the longest. She loves you like a daughter and for some reason she loves Mom, too."

"So?"

"Her son went into the Navy."

"I know that."

"She's lonely in her apartment without him. Says she's thinking of moving upstate to be with her sister. Get out of the city, fresh air, yada, yada, yada."

"Oh, my God." Kira's brain went into overdrive. "What will I do without Tippy?"

"See?" Krissy slapped her palm on the table. "That's your problem. Right away you're so worried about your precious schedule of coverage that you're missing out on a potential opportunity."

"And what might that be?"

"Now hear me out." She held up both hands. "What if you decide to move up to Westchester?"

"I can't—"

Krissy held up a finger. "I said to hear me out, now listen. I could tell how much you loved managing Derrick's office. You were damn good at it, too. What if you moved up there? What if you asked Tippy to move in with you as a live-in caregiver? That would get her out of her apartment filled with memories of her son. She wouldn't be lonely. She'd be in the country."

"Someplace with a fenced-in yard." Kira warmed to the idea. "Where Mom could get outside and maybe have a garden."

"That's right," Krissy said, nodding dreamily, as if lost in a memory. "I remember Mom saying one day she wanted to move to the country so she could have a big beautiful garden."

If only. Kira shook her head. "This is silly." To hope. To allow herself to dream of something she could never have. "So many things would have to happen for me to be able to pull that off. Even if I could, Derrick probably hates me anyway." Her heart twitched uncomfortably at the thought.

"He doesn't hate you," Krissy said.

How could she be so sure?

"All I'm suggesting," she went on. "Is rather than flat out saying no, it will never work, give you and Derrick and a future together some more thought. And you, uh," she stood and carried her dishes to the sink, "may want to figure it out sooner rather than later."

"Why?" Kira stacked Mom's plate and utensils onto her own plate.

"Because...I'm leaving."

Kira shot out of her chair. "You're what? When?" Kira had gotten used to having her around. "Why?" When they were finally starting to get along?

"First time's a charm," Krissy said, holding her arms out at her sides. "I'm pregnant."

Kira knew she should be happy for her sister but she just...couldn't...

"Don't look so sad," Krissy said. "This is a good thing." If it was so good, why did her smile look forced? "My friend Zac scored us two primo assignments on Oahu. Hawaii, baby." She made that hang loose sign with both hands and wiggled them. "I am going to have some fun in the sun while I can still rock my bikini."

"Krissy—"

"Three months with an option for three more." She slid the tips of her fingers into the front pockets of her tight jeans. "Then I'll come back to New York. I'll find a nice steady job that keeps me in one place, just like you want. I'll get my very own apartment where I will finally settle down as I prepare for motherhood."

She made it sound like she'd be serving out a sentence under house arrest. Which made no sense, didn't she want to be pregnant? "Krissy—"

Without waiting to hear what Kira had to say, Krissy turned and walked out of the kitchen toward the bedroom they were currently sharing.

Kira followed. "Krissy," she said again. "What about your job with Derrick?"

"That's all you're worried about?" She dropped down on her hands and knees to drag her duffle bag out from under her bed. "I'd thought for sure you'd get on me about prenatal care and not doing anything stupid while I'm pregnant." She stood and plopped the duffle onto the bed.

Kira let out a breath. "You're an adult and a nurse. I know you know you need good prenatal care. And I know you're responsible enough not to do anything stupid while you're pregnant." But maybe she should mention... "Like surfing. You probably shouldn't try surfing."

Krissy stopped, holding a stack of T-shirts she'd just taken out of her drawer, and smiled. "There's the overprotective sister I know and love."

"And heavy lifting," Kira added. "Make sure you get someone to help you with lifting."

"I will." Krissy packed the T-shirts in her duffle. "Don't worry about me. I promise to take good care of myself." She returned to the dresser and pulled open her pajama/sweats drawer. "As far as Derrick, I talked to him. He didn't have any problem with me leaving. Said he'd get along just fine. Frankly," she stopped what she was doing and looked at Kira. "I think I reminded him of you and he was glad to be rid of me."

"So you're done? You didn't even give him notice?"

Krissy shrugged. "I offered to stay on for a couple of more days, but he said no need. So I told Zac to book us on the first flight he could get." Her eyes met Kira's. "We're leaving tomorrow afternoon."

So soon? One more day? Then Krissy would be off on yet another adventure while Kira remained at home. Alone with Mom. And with Krissy gone, Kira knew she'd feel the loss of Derrick even more. She felt tears collecting in her eyes. She quickly turned so Krissy wouldn't see.

Her sister's arms came around her in a great big hug. "It's only for a few months." She squeezed. "Then I'll be back. Promise."

Too choked up to talk, all Kira could do was nod.

# CHAPTER SIXTEEN

On Thursday morning, before any of his staff arrived, Derrick sat out at the reception desk, looking over his schedule of patients, dreading the insanely busy day ahead and missing Kira. He stared down at a picture of her on his phone. She'd been asleep in his bed, so peaceful. He brought up another one of her sitting in the exact same spot where he was sitting, with a big, beautiful smile on her pretty face. His heart squeezed.

It hadn't even been two whole weeks, and he missed her so much. But he'd made it clear he wanted to try. She'd made it clear she didn't. If they were to have any hope of a future together, the next move would have to be hers.

He looked around the messy desk. Kira wouldn't have allowed it. He needed to find a new office manager, but couldn't bring himself to do it. A small, irrational part of him still clung to the hope that if the position remained open, maybe she'd come back to work...back to him.

Stupid.

And now he needed to find a nurse to replace Krissy, too.

God help him. Short-staffed again. Too much work. No fun. He'd come full circle.

Someone knocked on the glass door. Derrick looked up to see a thirtysomething woman with short blonde hair, wearing light blue scrub pants, a multicolored scrub top, and a pink stethoscope around her neck.

Was she lost? Derrick stood and answered the door. "May I help you?"

"My name is Andrea. My friends call me Andy." She held out her hand.

Derrick shook it.

Andrea went on, "A few weeks ago I brought my nephew in. He'd fallen off of his bike. You took him as a walk-in."

Derrick tried to place her, but couldn't.

"You were great with him. The staff was nice.

I'm new to the area so I talked with Kira to see if you had any RN work available. At the time she'd told me no, but she had me fill out an application."

Derrick started to feel a glimmer of hope.

"Anyway, she tracked me down last night to tell me a nursing position opened up, and if I could start immediately, it's mine." She held up a paper lunch sack. "So here I am."

Derrick's cell phone rang. He pulled it out of his pocket and glanced at the screen. Kira. "Come in." He invited Andrea in. Partly because it was the polite thing to do, partly so he could close the door with her inside so she wouldn't think about leaving. "Give me a minute to take this call."

"Sure thing."

Derrick accepted the call. "Hello?"

"It's Kira. Don't hang up."

"I know it's you," he said. "That's why I answered the call. What's up?"

"I have a nurse coming into the office today. Her name is Andrea. I already did her interview and checked her references. You can find the paperwork in the top drawer of my…of the file cabinet in my…in the office manager's office, in a file labeled Excellent Nursing Candidates. All you need to do is make a copy of her nursing license, which I told her to bring with her, and fill out the new hire paperwork that's in the same drawer in a file labeled New Hire Paperwork. I left a bunch of packets paper clipped together."

Typical Kira. So organized and right on top of things. Derrick couldn't help but smile. "She's already here."

"Oh. Sorry. I'd hoped to catch you before she arrived. But hey, she showed up early. That's a good thing."

"Yes it is."

"Tells you what kind of employee she'll be," Kira said. "I knew I liked her."

"I do, too."

The silence that followed grew awkward, until Kira broke it. "Well, that's it then."

Andrea stood a few feet away, looking around, trying to pretend she couldn't hear his every word. But Derrick wasn't ready to end the call.

He turned and walked to the far end of the waiting room. "How are you?"

"I'm doing well. How are you?"

"Better now that Andrea's here," he told her the truth.

"I'm glad."

She sounded glad for real. "Thank you for looking out for me," he said, touched by what she'd done.

"You're welcome."

He probably should have ended the call there but he couldn't say goodbye without letting her know, "I miss you."

She didn't respond at first, but then she said, "I miss you, too." Her voice so low he could hardly hear her.

More silence followed.

Derrick would have been content to stand there all day maintaining the connection between them. But he had so much to do. "I really need to—"

"Me, too."

"Call me sometime," he said before he could stop himself.

"Goodbye, Derrick."

He hated the finality of her tone.

"Goodbye."

Andrea proved to be a nice addition to his staff. She worked hard, got along well with Sara and Bonnie, and had no problem covering the reception desk when asked. His business thriving, he was making money and paying down his loans faster than he'd imagined possible. Sure, he worked his ass off, but what else did he have to do?

One week passed in a blur of patients and paperwork, then two, then three.

He got up to visit Mom and Dad once to see firsthand how well Mom was doing.

Kira never called.

He was finally getting used to life without her—to the point late one Saturday afternoon, after office hours, he'd pulled out her file labeled Excellent Office Manager Candidates and started looking for her replacement—when Krissy called.

Saturday night Kira sat at her kitchen table, sipping a glass of wine, scanning through the real estate listings she'd printed out at work, condos and small houses for sale within half an hour of Derrick's office. If she bought a house, she'd need to worry about mowing the grass in the summer and plowing snow from the driveway in the winter. A condo would be easier, but then Mom wouldn't have a private yard for her garden. Up in Westchester County she'd need a car, another expense. And she'd need to learn how to drive.

She took a few more sips, okay, more like large swallows of wine, then refilled her glass. It'd taken three weeks, but Kira, with Tippy's happy agreement to relocate with them, had figured out a doable plan that just might work. Assuming Derrick hadn't moved on. Assuming he still wanted her in his life and as his office manager.

"Three weeks." She took another sip of wine, staring at her phone. "Idiot." Why hadn't she called him? "Because you pushed him away and compared him to all the losers that'd come before him. He has every right to hate you now. And you're too much of a coward to call him, to admit you were wrong and you want another chance. Which is why you're sitting here talking to yourself rather than to him."

Last night, after refusing to discuss the topic during her prior phone calls with Krissy, Kira finally admitted that she'd never told Derrick of her plans to move so she could be closer to him. Why get his hopes up if she couldn't make it happen? And now, three weeks later, she was worried too much time had passed, that she'd missed her opportunity. Typical Krissy, she'd freaked out saying—

Someone knocked on her door.

Kira glanced at the clock. Who would be knocking at her door at eight o'clock at night? She stood, glanced into the living room to make sure Mom was occupied, then headed to the door. She looked through the peephole and sucked in a breath...could not believe her eye.

She opened the door.

There stood Derrick dressed as Debbie, carrying his briefcase.

"What are you doing here?"

"You going to let me in?" he asked in his Debbie voice.

Kira nodded and made room for him to enter.

Once inside Derrick said, "Krissy called. She said your mom was sick again and you were being too pigheaded to call me because you didn't want to bother me."

Sounded like something Krissy would do. Sweet, interfering Krissy.

"And you came?"

He stared deeply into her eyes as he cupped her cheek. "Of course I came. I'll always come if you need me. Never worry about bothering me."

God she loved him. Kira flung her arms around his neck. "Thank you."

He wrapped his arms around her waist and hugged her back. "So what's going on?"

Kira stepped back. "Nothing." She motioned into the living room. "Mom's fine. Watching television with the volume on low in a dimly lit room as usual."

"Then why—?"

"Come." Kira held out her hand. He took it

and she led him into the kitchen. "Can I get you something to drink?"

He eyed her glass of wine. "I'm driving so maybe a cup of coffee if you have?"

Kira opened the refrigerator. "Instant okay?"

"Instant's fine."

While Kira took out a mug, filled it with water and set it in the microwave, Derrick set his brief-case on the floor, pulled out a chair and took a seat at the table. "What's all this?"

Her back to him, Kira froze.

She heard him moving around the papers.

Well... She turned. Krissy had gotten him here, the rest was up to Kira. "I'm guessing all this," she pointed to the papers on the table, "is the rea-son Krissy had you come all the way down here. Because it'd been so long since we'd spoken and I was nervous to call you..."

"Houses in Mount Kisco? Somers? Golden's Bridge?"

The microwave pinged. Kira made Derrick's coffee like she had so many times at work. Then she put together a small plate of the Oreos she always kept on hand for Mom and delivered both to the table. "I guess none of that matters if you've filled your office manager position." Kira sat down across from him.

Eyes filled with caring, affection, and hope, met hers. "I haven't."

Thank you! "And would you be willing to keep it unfilled for a little while longer until I can find a place up in Westchester, sell my condo, and move Mom and me up there?"

Still staring at her, he nodded. "But what about your high-paying job with WCHC?"

Kira smiled. "Turns out I like the perks of working for you more than a big salary."

He slid his chair back and held out his arms. "Come here."

She didn't hesitate, straddling his lap, hugging him close. "God I've missed you."

He squeezed her tightly. "I've missed you, too." He pulled back to look at her. "So. Damn. Much." He moved some hair from the side of her face, then slid his hand to the back of her head, and pulled her in for a deep, loving, wonderful kiss.

"I smell Oreos," Mom called out from the other room.

Kira stiffened. Not now.

"Go," Derrick said.

"I'm sorry." Kira climbed off of his lap.

"Don't be."

She called out to Mom, "Be right there." Then to Derrick she said, "This is my life. Even with Tippy working as a live-in, she's going to need help, and time off. And I'll need to—"

"I understand, Kira," Derrick said. "I only wish I could help, that everything didn't fall on you."

How had she gotten so lucky? Kira took the package of Oreos down from the top shelf of the closet where she hid them. "After Mom gets settled in our new place, and I honestly have no idea how long that will take, maybe I can introduce a new caregiver. But even then—"

"I know what I'm getting into." Derrick stood. "I'm going into this relationship with my eyes wide open." He walked up behind her. "I can deal with sharing you." He leaned in and set a tender kiss on the side of her neck. "It's not having you in my life that's giving me trouble." He pressed in close. "Not having you in my bed." He thrust his pelvis against her butt. "Not seeing you every day or being able to talk with you."

"Oreos!" Mom yelled.

Kira turned in his arms, went up on her tippy toes and gave him a kiss on the cheek. "Hold that thought." She opened the refrigerator, grabbed the milk, and poured Mom a glass. "Be right back."

Mom taken care of, Kira returned to find Derrick leaning against the counter, still decked out as Debbie, waiting for her. She walked right into his arms, wrapping hers around his waist, setting her cheek to his chest. "I know there are no guarantees in life, but I need some assurance you're not going to change your mind, that you won't, at some point demand more than I can give you, that you—"

"I'm not going to change my mind—"

"Because I love you and I'm letting myself

think about a happy future, for the first time in a long time. A future with you and I know I'm getting totally ahead of myself, but maybe a baby. And if you have any concerns, any doubts..." She'd rather know now than have her heart broken later. "Because I'll be uprooting my life, and my mom's life. For you."

He lifted her chin and stared down into her eyes. "I have no doubts, Kira. I love you. I want you in my life, in my future." He sealed his words with a kiss. "I say we get working on that baby sooner rather than later." He thrust the bulge of his erection against her.

Kira laughed.

"That wasn't quite the reaction I was hoping for."

She laughed again. "It's your dress." She palmed his fake breasts. "And these."

He leaned in close to her ear and whispered, "Would you like to join me in your bedroom so I can take them off?"

Arousal surged through her system. She leaned against him. "You have no idea how much."

He thrust against her again, his erection even bigger and harder than before. Okay, maybe he did have an idea how much.

His hands caressed up her sides, stopping to cup her breasts before traveling back down to her butt. "When do you put your mother to bed?" He held her in place as he thrust his hips again. Lord help her.

Kira glanced at the clock. "Around ten." A whole hour and a half. "But maybe I can get started a little early tonight."

"You do that." He kissed her. Then, his lips still pressed to hers, he said, "I'll be waiting for you in your bed." As if that wasn't alluring enough he added, "Naked."

"I'll hurry." Kira turned to leave.

Derrick stopped her, reaching out to grab her arm. "Don't hurry," he said. "Do what you need to do. Take your time." He winked. "You're worth the wait."

In that instant Kira fell even more in love with him. He understood. He accepted that her mother had to come first. God willing, that would never change. "Thank you." She turned away, vowing from tonight on, she would make sure to always be worth the wait, so he would never stop waiting for her.

# EPILOGUE

*Six months later*

KIRA HUNG UP the phone.

"Everything okay?" Derrick asked, walking over to hand her a glass of wine.

Kira set it down on the counter. "Krissy was crying so hard all I could make out is the baby is fine and she'll be home tomorrow as planned." And something about Zac being a jerk and life sucking and a huge mistake. "Thank you for offering to drive me down to Newark Liberty International Airport to pick her up. I would have driven myself but…" Driving around town and to work was one thing. Down to a bustling airport? Not ready for that yet.

Derrick held up his beer mug in a toast. "Happy to do it." Then he returned to his seat on the couch and picked up the medical journal he'd been reading when the phone rang.

Kira looked around the home they'd purchased, decorated, and had been living in together for the past three weeks, happier than she'd ever been. After much research, they'd found the perfect mother-daughter setup with three bedrooms and two bathrooms in the main living area, and a private apartment with one large bedroom, that they divided into two, and a separate entrance for Mom and Tippy. With the money Kira got from selling her condo in the city, they were able to put down a big deposit and still have enough left over for all new furniture.

She walked over to the sliding door that led to the deck and stared out into their large yard. "They did a beautiful job on the fence." A high wooden privacy fence that split the yard in two so Derrick could have his fire pit and cornhole and Mom could go outside to garden any time she wanted.

Her fiancé of three weeks—he'd proposed with a beautiful ring on their first night in their new home—walked up behind her, pressed in close, and kissed her neck—something he did often. "Can't wait to get you out there for some drunk stargazing."

Sober stargazing would likely have to do for the next nine months. "As soon as the April showers head out and the ground dries." Kira leaned back against his firm, broad chest. "Are you sure you're okay with Krissy living here until she finds her own place?" Especially on account of she'd be working at the family practice, too.

"Your family is my family."

Poor man, he'd really taken on a lot when he'd taken on Kira. She turned in his arms and looked up at him. "There's something I've been putting off telling you."

He looked down at her with concern. "What?"

"It may be just stress from the move and work being so busy and all the problems I've been having getting Mom settled in. But…I'm late."

It took him a few seconds to figure out what that meant. "You mean?"

She nodded. "Our crazy family may be getting bigger."

He picked her up and spun her around.

Kira laughed. "So I take that to mean you're happy about the news?"

He walked them over to the couch and sat down, settling Kira in his lap. "I am ecstatic about the news." He smiled. Then he kissed her.

Kira was ecstatic, too. They'd only been together for a few months, but Derrick had already given her a future filled with more happiness than she'd thought possible. "Thank you for coming down to the city to yell at me." She shifted around until she was straddling his lap, one of her favorite places to be.

"I didn't—"

She put her finger to his lips. "Yes, you did."

He smiled. "You're right. I did."

"And thank you for following me to that bar, and dragging me up to your parents' house, and coming to my condo when Mom was sick." She rocked along the growing length of him. "Thank you for loving me enough to put up with a life that includes my mother and my sister."

He started to move beneath her.

"Thank you for giving me a job I love that makes it possible for me to spend so much time with the man I love." She leaned in and kissed him.

"I love you, too." He held her tightly. "Now let's go to the bedroom so I can show you how much."

He showed her every day, in *and* out of the bedroom. Kira climbed off of his lap. "Bet I can make you come first."

Derrick scooped her up into his arms and ran down the hall. "Bet I can make *you* come first."

Twenty minutes later, Derrick won. And Kira was perfectly okay with that.

\* \* \* \* \*

*Look out for the next great story in the*
NURSES TO BRIDES *duet*
*THE NURSE'S NEWBORN GIFT.*

*And if you enjoyed this story, check out these
other great reads from Wendy S. Marcus:*

*NYC ANGELS: TEMPTING NURSE SCARLET
CRAVING HER SOLDIER'S TOUCH
SECRETS OF A SHY SOCIALITE
THE NURSE'S NOT-SO-SECRET SCANDAL*

*All available now!*

# MILLS & BOON®
## Large Print Medical

## March

| | |
|---|---|
| A Daddy for Her Daughter | Tina Beckett |
| Reunited with His Runaway Bride | Robin Gianna |
| Rescued by Dr Rafe | Annie Claydon |
| Saved by the Single Dad | Annie Claydon |
| Sizzling Nights with Dr Off-Limits | Janice Lynn |
| Seven Nights with Her Ex | Louisa Heaton |

## April

| | |
|---|---|
| Waking Up to Dr Gorgeous | Emily Forbes |
| Swept Away by the Seductive Stranger | Amy Andrews |
| One Kiss in Tokyo... | Scarlet Wilson |
| The Courage to Love Her Army Doc | Karin Baine |
| Reawakened by the Surgeon's Touch | Jennifer Taylor |
| Second Chance with Lord Branscombe | Joanna Neil |

## May

| | |
|---|---|
| The Nurse's Christmas Gift | Tina Beckett |
| The Midwife's Pregnancy Miracle | Kate Hardy |
| Their First Family Christmas | Alison Roberts |
| The Nightshift Before Christmas | Annie O'Neil |
| It Started at Christmas... | Janice Lynn |
| Unwrapped by the Duke | Amy Ruttan |

# MILLS & BOON®
## Large Print Medical

## June

| | |
|---|---|
| **White Christmas for the Single Mum** | Susanne Hampton |
| **A Royal Baby for Christmas** | Scarlet Wilson |
| **Playboy on Her Christmas List** | Carol Marinelli |
| **The Army Doc's Baby Bombshell** | Sue MacKay |
| **The Doctor's Sleigh Bell Proposal** | Susan Carlisle |
| **Christmas with the Single Dad** | Louisa Heaton |

## July

| | |
|---|---|
| **Falling for Her Wounded Hero** | Marion Lennox |
| **The Surgeon's Baby Surprise** | Charlotte Hawkes |
| **Santiago's Convenient Fiancée** | Annie O'Neil |
| **Alejandro's Sexy Secret** | Amy Ruttan |
| **The Doctor's Diamond Proposal** | Annie Claydon |
| **Weekend with the Best Man** | Leah Martyn |

## August

| | |
|---|---|
| **Their Meant-to-Be Baby** | Caroline Anderson |
| **A Mummy for His Baby** | Molly Evans |
| **Rafael's One Night Bombshell** | Tina Beckett |
| **Dante's Shock Proposal** | Amalie Berlin |
| **A Forever Family for the Army Doc** | Meredith Webber |
| **The Nurse and the Single Dad** | Dianne Drake |